The Cave of Treasure

By Jeff R. Smith

and

Richard Roux

Riverview Books

Published by Riverview Books

Sandpoint, ID

Copyright © 2019 by Jeff R. Smith & Richard Roux

Cover art by Emilie Beck

All Rights Reserved

ISBN-13: 978-0-578-59184-1

For Dwayne Bishop, Scott Pierce, Craig Roberts, and
Norm Reimers. Friends, brothers, and mentors. Knowing
you, then and now, has made us better humans.

CONTENTS

Acknowledgments   i

1   1

2   31

3   44

4   60

5   74

6   93

7   116

8   124

9   138

10   161

11   170

ACKNOWLEDGMENTS

I would like to thank my wife Sherri for her patience, love, and support throughout the process of my writing, as well as for her editing. She is always the first to work on my books after I'm done typing them.

I want to thank my children for putting up with my constant talking about whatever project I'm working on at the time. My youngest says he is going to write a book, too.

I would like to thank the rest of my family (you know who you are) for supporting my work, even if they don't think the same way as I do.

I would also like to give a big thanks to my fans out there. Without you, this would just be me telling a story to those in my home.

Last but not least, I would like to thank my friend Richard for making this book so much better than the manuscript I originally gave him. He and I used to stay up late at night playing fantasy games when we were...well, young.

1

The short, young lad stroked his freshly oiled brick red beard as he walked into his parents' store. His mom and dad were focused on the various crates and bags before them, reaffirming that the shipment contained all that it should.

Standing before his parents, the young man waited for his opportunity to speak. He was nervous, but he'd rehearsed in his head what he wanted to say for several weeks. The time had come for him to speak.

"Father, ma, it's nearly my fiftieth birthday," he said to his parents as they both looked in his direction.

He took a deep breath and then confidently said, "I want to go out and kill Orcs for a living."

His father sighed and looked at him sternly. He was annoyed with his son's persistence, a fact that was reflected in the tone of his voice and gestures he made with his hands.

"We have talked of this before. Until you are an adult, you will stay here and mind your manners."

In a quick, fluid motion, the young Dwarf kneeled on his right knee in a sign of respect and obedience to his father.

With a calmness in his voice the young man looked at his father in the eye, stating, "Yes father, of course. I will stay the few extra days until one day after adulthood, but then I will be off in search of my destiny."

He stood back up to his 4ft 9 1/2 in, walked over to his mother, hugged, and kissed her on the left cheek. His footsteps seemed to echo as he walked out of the store. Glad to have that task over, he turned onto the main underground hall that many used every day. Dain Stonefist had another stop to make this day, and he was excited to reach the destination.

Dain headed down Glitter Hall for nearly a half mile, not really noticing all the other shops he was so used to seeing, nor did he give much notice to the patrons and clerks who chatted and bartered. He was focused on the task at hand. It wasn't long before he took a smaller road that led down into the lower Deeps of the city.

After descending two levels of faintly lit and slightly damp tunnel road, he passed a group of City Guard escorting three silver haired, tall, skinny folks from the forest.

What are the weaseling Elves doing down here? Dain thought to himself. *They're not good for anything more than fighting practice!* He huffed in disgust, thinking, *They're only a small step above Orcs...and both are sworn enemies!* But today he kept walking.

He had more important things to do. Today he would finally get to see his new best friend. Dain continued, giving the trio of forest folks one last thought. *Besides, the City Guard could carve them up easily.*

He continued down three more levels before finally reaching his destination. The proprietor was making quite the racket while sorting through a crate of damaged weapons when Dain walked in.

"Mr. Shellback?" Dain announced his presence.

The older man briskly turned, doing his best to mask being startled.

"Ah, Dain my boy, I've been waiting for you."

He motioned to Dain to wait a moment as he walked over to the far wall and hefted a large double-headed battle axe from the floor. The sound of grating metal on the stone-cobbled floor sang throughout the room. Mr. Shellback hefted the battle axe and presented it to Dain.

"This is one of the best pieces I've ever made. It has an Ironwood handle and the blades are sharp enough to shave with, yet strong enough to last a lifetime. You may need to get used to its weight...it's much heavier than a normal one."

With a smile on his bearded face, Dain took the offered weapon with his left hand, easily hoisting it into the air.

"It doesn't feel heavy to me, just very stout, as I asked,"

Dain chuckled.

Mr. Shellback's eyebrows arched, first in astonishment, and then in understanding. He rubbed his chin as he responded to Dain.

"Yes son, I tend to forget that you have the strength of your father." He laughed thinking about Dain's strength, stating, "There are not many even amongst us Dwarves that have the strength of a Giant, yet you have proven it many times."

Dain felt pride in the complement and recognition that he was an exceptional specimen of the Dwarf race.

"I thank you for your fine work. This axe will serve me well," Dain graciously responded to Mr. Shellback.

"So," Mr. Shellback inquired, "are you leaving tomorrow as you planned?"

Dain frowned and shook his head. "No, my father has forbidden it. I will wait until I am fifty plus one day." A slight annoyance could be detected in his voice.

"Well, I suppose your father has his reasons and knows best," Mr. Shellback reasoned. "But on the bright side, you'll soon be on your way!"

With a last thought before Dain took his leave, Mr. Shellback licked his lips and excitedly stated, "I've been looking forward to the day of feasting I know your mother will have for you."

****

"Out! Out! And never come back here again!" the Sheriff yelled at poor misunderstood Dinly.

If only she could have taken the loaf of cake with her the scolding would have been more tolerable. The least the Sheriff could do was lock her up again and feed her for a while. It was difficult to live when you had no money, no job, no home, and no food. Poverty was a lonely and hungry enterprise.

Dinly dejectedly walked off into the nearby woods and recovered the pack she earlier hid amidst some brush and boulders. Alone, and surmising her situation, she opened the pack to take stock of her belongings.

This is all I have. My pack, a half-used flint and steel, two water flasks, a dagger, a blanket, the clothing on my back, and two lock picks. Oh, almost forgot...I do have a completely empty purse. Her thoughts reflected the downtrodden countenance she momentarily had.

She looked from the woods toward the town the Sheriff had just banned her from. A wagon slowly rolled down the road heading toward one of the few businesses located in the small town where her family of Halflings used to live. There were still Halflings there, but none were her kin. Her family was long gone.

Those nasty Baldfeet taking over things, she angrily thought to herself.

Driven by hunger, Dinly refused to comply with the Sheriff. She deftly walked out of the woods and back into town, melding within the shadows as much as possible. As she rounded the corner of the General Store, she saw the wagon stop, confirming her guess that it was hauling supplies.

Her eyes flitted from the wagon to the store, and up and down the mostly vacant road. *Where is the driver?* she thought. Her assessment prompted her conclusion. *Probably in the store.*

Dinly took in her surroundings and the situation. With her trained eye she spied several bags that could have smoked meat in them, and there was a partial loaf of bread on the driver's seat. Hearing the two men talking inside, she seized the opportunity and dashed to the wagon. In an instance, Dinly grabbed both the nearest bag and the partial loaf, turned, and then retraced her steps. Her feeling of accomplishment was short-lived.

"Hey, you!" a man yelled from inside the General Store. "Hey! Stop right there!"

Dinly knew what was at stake as she ran back toward the forest. She ran as fast as her little legs would move, not heeding the temptation to look back. She dipped and dodged over logs, around boulders, and through brush until she reached better cover amidst the trees where she hazarded a quick glance back toward the man who was yelling and pursuing her. The driver chased her about a hundred feet, threw up his hands in disgust, and stopped. He realized pursuing the thief was an exercise in futility. Dinly laughed a girlish laugh and kept running until she knew she couldn't be seen. It was then that she felt safe enough to stop and rest.

"Let's see what I grabbed," she whispered out loud to herself as she untied the drawstrings on the bag.

As she opened the bag the smell of the contents betrayed the cloth and gave rise to her disappointment.

"Fish?" she exclaimed. "Smoked Fish!" Dinly's disgust and disappointment couldn't be disguised, nor quieted.

"Yuck! Why couldn't I have picked up a roast or a ham? Oh well, it's still better than nothing...barely. I guess it will have to do."

She took a piece of the fish out of the bag, bit off a chunk of the firm flesh, and tried to savor its taste. Hardly satisfied, she continued to think about her predicament. *I need to find a new place to live or find a job somewhere far from town.* She continued to chew the smoky fish as she investigated the bag. *There's enough fish in here to get me to Windy Dale. I guess this is my chance.*

Dinly walked over to a nearby stream and sank her empty water flask to fill it up. She took a big drink from her other flask before topping it off. It was best to gather when it was plentiful. Careful not to slip, she walked across a fallen log covered in moss, and headed in the direction of Windy Dale. Mindful of events earlier in the evening, Dinly made sure she wouldn't come out of the forest where she might run into the delivery driver on his way back from where he came. That would be problematic.

****

The young woman was giddy with excitement. She had just completed her tutorial training at the School of Wizardry and was now an apprentice. After years of being alone and feeling like an outcast, she finally felt accepted by someone.

Until the last two years, Trina Haywood had lived a life mostly filled with tragedy. When she was eight years old, Trina lost both of her parents. It was a heartbreaking situation, that could have been worse if not for the fact that her only remaining relatives, her aunt and uncle on her father's side, took her in and provided refuge. What could have been a life salvaged turned into a nightmare after two years. Trina's aunt and uncle both died by the hands of slavers, leaving her, once again, all alone. Added to the emotional anguish of losing another set of guardians, she was kidnapped by those very slavers and forced into bondage.

Her life as a slave lasted just over seven arduous years. It was her good fortune that a group of adventurers happened along and wiped out the band of Half-Orcs that had bought her from the slavers. That band of adventurers developed an affinity for Trina, touched by her plight and what it had done to her life. Since the adventurers' journey had been especially lucrative, they decided to grant Trina a new life. They were willing to help her in whatever way they could. Trina told them she'd like to attend Wizardry School, and to her delight, each adventurer pitched in enough money to pay for her to go to the School for two years.

Two of the adventurers came by to see her a month ago, and they were allowed a short visit. Trina informed them that she could stay at the school until the day after her evaluation. After that, her destiny was unwritten. One of the team members suggested that Trina would have a job if she wanted it. All she needed to do was to meet them at the Longtree Tavern.

Her interest piqued; Trina told the lady that she was very much interested in hearing the offer. Trina examined the woman as she talked with her in the dorm room. The woman had a kind, if not worldly-looking, Elven face, with long golden hair, and a strange cloak. Trina thought about the offer, contemplating her place in this world as the woman left. She wasn't sure what she wanted to do, but one thing for sure was that her time at the Wizardry School here was over.

Left with her thoughts, Trina walked to her bed and packed her possessions. There wasn't much, just a small Spell Book, various Spell Components, an extra robe, a waterproof hooded cloak, and a candle. Except for the staff that was leaning against the wall by her bed, all her items went into a backpack. *This is it*, she thought. *This is all I own*.

Trina was brought back to reality when she heard the ringing of the dinner bell. It was the last dinner she'd have at the School.

****

The Longtree Tavern was a cozy establishment tucked along the main road running through the village. It would be difficult to miss, what with the shouts and raucous laughter emanating from the building. Rumor had it that the Tavern was the best place to go if you were looking for an adventuring party to join or if you already had a party, but needed one or two additional skilled individuals to flush your numbers. It also had a reputation as being the toughest place in town. There were fights almost every night. In fact, it was easier for the patrons to recall when the last brawl was than when there wasn't one.

An Elven lady walked through the door in an outfit that left very little to the imagination, quickly looked over the room, and then went straight to the bar.

"Well...you look lost! What can I do for you?" the bartender curiously asked.

The woman scoffed, "I'm not lost, sir. Do you have a larger door for a friend of mine to enter through?"

This caught the bartender off guard because of the odd nature of the question. With a somewhat confused look on his face he shook his head.

"No ma'am I…"

But he didn't get a chance to finish his thought before a burly man with five friends called out in a forceful tone from a table in the middle of the room.

"Hey woman! We only put up with your kind here if we get to spend some quality time with you, so you better get over here!"

The men around the table burst out in jovial laughter. It wasn't because the man was joking, but more out of the fact that they knew what pleasures they were to have with this Elven woman.

"I'm sorry ma'am," the bartender quietly said before he was interrupted again.

The burly man stood up and the once lively room went quiet.

"Hey wench, I'm talkin' to you!"

Undeterred, the woman continued to face the bartender when she replied to the man in an elevated volume.

"I'm no wench and I'm trying to converse with this gentleman here. Please, just mind your manners!"

Not used to being disobeyed, the burly man started walking toward her. He was clearly irritated and more than willing to push the issue. He was shouting now, with spittle flying from his lips.

"If I say you're a wench, then you're a wench! I run this town!"

He grabbed for her with a large, calloused hand only to find that she easily dodged his efforts. He reached for her again with the same results, except with lightning speed she grabbed the man's outstretched arm and pulled it behind his back.

"Get her boys!" he called out in discomfort.

Unbeknownst to the man and his cronies, the lady had a friend outside that was keeping a close watch on what was happening inside. He knew his Elven companion could handle a normal man on any given day of the week, but when the other five goons stood up and started toward her, he didn't like her odds. His enormous frame smashed through the doorway and headed to intercept them.

The sound of splintering wood and flying debris immediately stopped the men in their tracks. There, in what used to be the doorway, the men saw through the dust the silhouette a huge man. He was an impressive sight at around eight feet tall and close to 600 lbs. of solid muscle. And in the same sense he was terrifying, especially since that giant of a man was coming straight at them and they collectively froze in their tracks. He dropped his maul onto the floor with a crashing thud where it fell through the wooden plank floor to the dirt ground below the building. Without hesitation, he began punching the five men in front of him. He only had to hit each man once to put them out of commission. Two of the men were able to hit the large man, but it was no use. They hurt their hands and were knocked unconscious before they knew what else they should do.

As the last man fell to the floor the large man turned his attention to the ringleader restrained by the Elf. The wide-eyed burly man was begging for her to let go, and as a grin spread over the large man's face and his gaze fixed on the burly man who looked tiny in comparison, the Elf felt the fight go out of him quickly and let go in the hope that the man had learned his lesson.

The Giant took a couple of steps and retrieved his maul, pulling it from the collapsed floor. He looked over at the barkeep, slightly frowned and shrugged his shoulders.

"Sorry about your floor," he said in a deep voice that reverberated the insides of the barkeep, "but if me don't drop maul and used it on dose guys, day be dead."

Incredulous, the barkeep looked at the Giant to what used to be the doorway, and then back to the Giant. He did this a few times before he turned back to the Elf.

Exasperated, the barkeep pleaded with the Elf, "What about my doorway?"

Nonchalantly, as if she'd done this before, she pulled out a plump bag of coins that jingled as she untied the straps.

"Make it bigger," she instructed as she dropped several gold coins onto the bar top.

"Yes ma'am," he stammered. "What...what about the hole in my floor?"

"Don't push it," the Elf warned as she secured the opening of the sack with the leather straps. "There is more than enough there to cover any costs you may have."

The barkeep was eager to avoid further conflict.

"Okay, can't blame a guy for trying."

She gave him a look of disgust. "We'll be waiting for someone in that corner over there, and the money I gave you will also cover our food and drink."

The Elf grabbed the hilt of her sword to punctuate her words.

"It would behoove you to *not* add any extra ingredients to what you bring us." She nodded toward the Giant and added, "My friend is immune to them and you don't want him mad at you."

The barkeep took a step backward and raised his hands pleadingly as he said, "Of course, of course, the thought never crossed my mind! What will you have? Anything...just tell me! The list is on that wall." He pointed to his right.

She looked over the menu keeping in mind her friend's larger-than-life appetite. To play it safe, she ordered on the generous side.

"We'll take three bowls of beef stew with cornbread, three legs of lamb, and we'll follow that with a cherry pie. I'll have a sealed bottle of white wine and four tankards of your best ale for him."

He took a deep breath as the Elf rattled off her order and then rubbed his temple as he did some math.

"The cheap wine is gone, and I'd have to get a pricey bottle if you want a sealed bottle of white." His voice betrayed his nervousness as he finished, "Even with what you gave me, I'd have to ask for at least an additional seven silver rounds."

Fed up, but somewhat understanding, she pulled out a silver bar from the hefty coin bag and slapped it on the bar top. "That's worth ten silver rounds, don't ask for more."

"Yes ma'am," the barkeep answered as he retrieved the silver bar and scurried away.

She gave her friend a look and they started toward a table in a dark corner. The Giant grabbed one of the six chairs surrounding the table where the unconscious men on the floor were sitting as he followed the Elf.

"Man won't need no more," he stated to nobody in particular.

As he placed it next to another chair in the corner and began to sit on them, two of the men on the floor started to stir. The burly man was still sulking near the bar but was starting to become angry over the embarrassment he brought onto himself. He walked over and helped his buddies, including a third man after the first two were finally up off the floor. Two of the men were still out cold. The four of them, one who had his ego injured and the other three still feeling groggy from being punched-out, straightened out their clothes and gear, picked the two men on the floor up by their hands and legs, and then carried out them outside.

The lady noticed the looks the men shot their way and commented to her large friend, "You know, those guys are going to be a problem until we get rid of them permanently."

"Then those men dumber than me," the Giant remarked.

In some ways that statement was true, in others, not so much. The big man was incredibly strong, almost as strong as his father, but he wasn't blessed with much in the intelligence department and he knew it. Throughout his life, several people had told him so, and they had done so in many cruel ways. Most of them would never pick on anyone else ever again.

Ever since the first moment he had met his female companion, the Giant felt appreciated. He hadn't felt that way since leaving home. From that moment on, for more than seven years now, they had been an inseparable team. He would always say, "She got smarts...me protect her smarts."

It took both serving wenches two trips each to bring the food and drink to the table, and one of the women almost tripped over the gigantic maul. The huge man was nice enough to set it down gently when he took his seat in order to not make another hole in the floor, but it was hard not for it to be in the way. One would think that the weight of the maul, plus the weight of the man's nearly 600 lbs., would surely make the man fall through the floor, but the weapon was only heavy when he wasn't holding it. In his hands, it was no heavier than a normal war hammer. It was one of two items his father had given him when he left home. The other was a magically shrunk and protected portrait of his mother who had been kidnapped in his youth and never seen again.

One of the rather busty serving wenches, apparently the lead server, turned toward the two patrons after setting the food and drink down on the table.

"Is there anything else we can get you?"

"A wine glass would be nice, and maybe a couple of clean napkins," The Elven lady replied.

"Very well...coming right up."

As the Elf waited for her glass and napkins, she heard raised voices coming from the other side of the now open doorway to the tavern. It sounded like "Mr. burly" was at it again. *Oh well*, she thought, *let him be obnoxious to some others.* She and her large friend were more interested in eating and drinking in peace.

The head wench brought the glass and napkins to the table and set it down. Pleased, the Elven lady gave her two silver rounds, one for each of the two servers.

"Oh, thank you gracious lady, thank you!"

The serving wenches were only paid a silver round a day, plus tips, which usually consisted of two to five copper rounds. As the head wench, she earned an extra two copper rounds a day. Because of the woman's generosity, she and her son would eat a tiny bit of meat and cheese with dinner tonight.

"If you need anything else my lady, anything at all, you just let me know."

"I'll keep that in mind."

The head wench went to the other server, urged her into the kitchen, and gave her the other silver round where other workers couldn't see. Their excitement was barely contained. They both looked out the kitchen door to the dark table in the corner where the huge man and woman dug into their meal. *Who are they?* the two women wondered.

****

Trina Haywood walked down the street searching for the Longtree Tavern. She was to meet the man and woman that had freed her from the slavers and sent her to school. According to their arrangements, it was the correct time and day, and she hoped the two would already be there. Despite being able to now use magic, the tavern's reputation for day and night rough and tumble situations made her nervous.

After a few minutes of searching, Trina located the establishment, but before she had the chance to enter, her attention was drawn to a young girl surrounded by rough looking men. During her years as a slave, she had been treated badly, and her ability to empathize with the oppressed was heightened. With no help in sight, and seeing this little girl being harassed, Trina's temper flared. It continued to fester as she approached and was now close enough to hear the conversation.

"…not looking for trouble," the girl pleaded.

"Then just hand over what we asked for and let me and the boys spend some time with you…then you can go free."

The words resonated within Trina's memory. She had been told something similar once, before she was enslaved. Right before.

"Then I won't have anything more than the clothes on my back!" she protested. "I'll not give what few possessions I have away willingly!"

Enraged, the man loudly stated, "Then I guess we'll just have to take what we want instead of asking politely again! Either way, we will have what we want!"

By this time Trina had arrived. She wasn't going to leave this girl to the dogs.

"I think you should leave the girl alone!" Trina firmly stated.

The men in front of Trina parted, allowing her to move next to the girl.

Oh no! Trina immediately thought. *This isn't a girl at all...it's a female Halfling!*

The men closed ranks around both women. Trina realized too late that both she and the Halfling were now surrounded.

"Well now, looky here boys," the burly man cockily blurted. "It looks like twice the fun tonight!"

The other men chuckled, making the evil smiles on their faces even more grotesque, even though some of those faces looked like they had already lost a fight that night.

People on both sides of the street stopped to watch what was going on, the way a crowd gathers to witness a tragedy unfold. Only one man...a short man...kept moving, looking like he didn't even notice anything was amiss.

"I must warn you," Trina announced, "I just graduated from the School of Wizardry here in town, and you won't like how this ends up for you!"

With her attention diverted, the man behind her easily grabbed her and held her arms and hands to her sides and kicked away her staff.

How could I have done something so foolish? Trina thought in a panic.

****

Dain Stonefist was elated. Not only had his fiftieth birthday gone well for the family, but he was given several gifts that were truly helpful over the past four days of travel. Family and friends gave him some solid boots for hiking, a helm that actually fit his head, two flasks for drink (giving him a total of four), torches, candles, and a cooking pan. His uncle gave him a sturdy shield to protect himself in time of need, and his mother told him she would have food ready for his trip. It was enough to last him a couple of weeks. Since he spent his entire savings on the battle axe, she gave him a little money for the road.

Surprisingly, he received nothing from his father that day. It wasn't until he was packing to leave on the second morning after his birthday that his father asked him to come with him. They went into his father's War Room, where his father presented him with an old suit of scale armor that his father had worn during the Goblin Wars back when Dain was only thirty years old. He could see that the armor had been cleaned and had all new attaching leather.

"Let's adjust this to fit you so you can wear it during your travels," his father had said with a mixture of pride and sadness. "The closest place to meet others wanting to band together as a team would be the Longtree Tavern in Windy

Dale."

Dain thought quickly.

"Isn't that about three days march from here?"

"Yes son, it is...and you'd be better received if you were open to people of all races when you get there. There aren't as many Dwarves leaving the mountains these days with all the mining going on and the two new clans starting up."

Grateful for the gift of armor and the advice, Dain responded, "Okay father, I'll keep that in mind."

So here he was, walking up to the tavern his father told him about. Oddly enough, it was a tavern with no door, just a gaping hole in the side of the structure. He noticed several men and women heatedly talking in front of the entrance. It was none of his business, and he started to go around them to enter the Tavern, when he overheard one woman speak.

"…just graduated from the School of Wizardry here in town. You won't like how this ends up for you!"

Then he heard a man order, "Let's take them to the hideout boys!"

To Dain, this sounded like a kidnapping. Even if they weren't Dwarves, he didn't think kidnapping women was something he could let slide.

"Excuse me there fellas, but you wouldn't be trying to take these ladies against their will now, would ya?" Dain asked.

"Beat it shorty! This is no business of yours!" a burly man, for a Human, told Dain.

Dain thought about that statement for a fraction of a moment, and then squinted his eyes in his growing anger.

"You know...you're right. It's not my business, but you went and called me shorty, which is an insult to me! That is certainly my business!"

Dain swung his axe before any of the men could react, cleaving the man to his right clean in two. He cut through the second man before the others had their weapons out. Muscle, and bone, and blood painted the macabre portrait.

With one man still holding Trina, that left three to one odds, but they forgot about the Halfling, Dinly, until she used her dagger to sever the spine of the man nearest to her from behind.

The burly man turned to attack the Halfling as Dain hit the other man's sword so hard with his axe that the sword shattered. The axe continued its downward swing enough to cut a slight furrow into the man's flesh.

Fearing for his life, the man holding Trina let go and started to run away. A slight feeling of static electricity filled the air as Trina promptly cast a spell that threw several red points of light at the running man. The points of light hit the man with crushing, burning force, killing him before he hit the ground.

The burly man with the big mouth was now surrounded by the three of them, and there was no help in sight.

"I surrender!" he called out.

Dain spoke, "Men like you only surrender until they can, again, get other people to do their dirty work. Then, you are just how you were a few minutes ago. In my culture, you're already dead, but this is not my town."

He looked at all the bystanders and sought a verdict.

"What say you?" Dain inquired of the crowd.

A loud shout of "KILL HIM! OFF WITH HIS HEAD!" and other such things were called out by many.

"Do you have a town constable here?" Dain asked the collective crowd.

An older woman, full of vengeance, walked up and spit in the face of the burly man.

"Not since he killed my husband a few weeks ago. Since then, he and his men take what they want, rape who they want, and have taken many young women away to never be seen again."

Dain had an idea as he looked down at the injured man on the ground.

"Do you know where this hideout is, or are you worthless to me?"

Hoping to give the Dwarf a reason to spare his life, the

man quickly answered, "Yes! Yes, I know where it is!"

It sounded more like he was begging than giving affirmation to the Dwarf's question.

"Good!" Trina spoke, and then promptly conjured a spell that killed the burly man. "I hate bullies and slavers."

Dain was impressed by her decisiveness.

"That was what I'd call swift justice. My name is Dain...Dain Stonefist."

"My name is Trina Haywood, and I thank you for your help."

Dain gave a slight bow to Trina and then turned toward the Halfling.

"And your name would be what, miss?" Dain asked.

"I am called Dinly, and my surname is Gleaner," the Halfling answered. "I came here to find a company that might take me in when these ruffians tried to waylay me. Thank you both for helping me."

"Funny you should say that," Dain added. "I came here for the same reason. How about you Trina?"

"I am supposed to meet two friends here. They freed me from slavery and put me through the Wizardry School here for two years."

Dain, satisfied with the small talk and concluding that he'd found some new friends, walked to the bodies heaped on the ground and began to remove items.

"Well, the first thing we need to do is strip these bodies of anything useful," Dain stated.

He looked to see that the locals were staying well away from the bodies. It is a fool that tries to get something from the dead if they are not part of the unit that killed them in the first place. This is especially true if they can't defeat the victors that did.

"You two watch him and his dead friends while I go retrieve the body of the runner," Dain ordered politely.

Within minutes, the dead bodies and the injured man were stripped of any useful possessions, although the injured man was allowed to wear his boots and clothing. They gathered swords and daggers with scabbards, purses and money, good boots, some leather armor, flasks, bags, a couple of keys, and some other small items.

"Not a bad haul for a couple minutes of fun!" Dain called out. "We've got the prisoner patched up. What do you say we go inside and get a bite to eat?"

Dinly was hungry and eagerly consented.

"Anything but fish!"

"Don't like fish?" Trina asked.

"Not after eating it and nothing else for days on end!"

Dain and Trina both laughed. Dinly didn't think it was much of an amusing statement, but she joined in with a faux laugh of her own.

"Okay...for you, no fish," Dain compromised.

The three of them walked in, loaded down with weapons, armor, and other gear, all the while leading the prisoner. Trina noticed her friends in a dark corner, and she motioned to her new friends.

"There they are," and Trina started walking toward them.

Dain and Dinly both started to follow Trina, but then hesitated at the sight of the huge man sitting on two chairs. They resumed following only after Trina's assurances that it was okay.

"Hello Trina, "the lady asked. "Who are your friends?"

She introduced her new friends, and then Trina, Dain, and Dinly all grabbed empty chairs after setting down their loads and putting the prisoner against the wall where they could easily see him. Trina told the story of what happened outside.

The huge man looked over at the prisoner and taunted in a deep tone, "You die real bad."

Fear and resignation gripped the prisoner, and he could no longer control his bladder.

When Trina got to the part where Dain's axe shattered the sword, Dain couldn't refrain from interjecting.

"Put a slight burr in my blade, it did!"

When the story was finished, the Elven lady introduced

herself as Terelle.

Sensing it was the right thing to do, the Giant chimed in, "Me Splat, 'cause me splat 'em!"

After introductions were completed, Terelle called over one of the serving wenches and ordered food and drink for the other three, with NO FISH. She had mercy on the prisoner and ordered him water.

When the food was ready, the bartender helped the wenches bring it all to the table.

"How much will all of this cost?" Terelle asked, prepared to pay for it all.

"Normally this would come to five silver rounds, but considering that your friends here just disposed of the thief that was extorting me and causing such a problem for all of us...it's on the house," the bartender proudly announced.

"Thank you very much!" Dinly beamed. "Boy, I haven't had cornbread in years!"

She took a big bite and emanated sounds of contentment as she worked her way through a second piece.

After the food was consumed, Terelle settled everyone down to make an announcement.

"You know, with all of you and the two of us, we'd be a pretty formidable team." She paused a moment to let the statement sink in.

"What do you all say about getting you geared up

properly, and then have dumbo there," she nodded toward the prisoner, "show us this hideout?"

One by one they all voted in favor, even the Dwarf who wasn't supposed to like Elves such as Terelle. They were all in, except for the prisoner, of course.

2

Terelle called over the Head Wench.

"Yes Ma'am, is there something I can get you?"

"Yes, we need information, and I have faith that I can trust in you," Terelle confided. "Which merchant in this village is the least likely to try to rip us off?"

"They all will," the wench said with a sigh, "but one of them is a cousin of mine. If I send a note with you, he won't completely steal you blind, especially when I let him know who you got rid of."

Pleased with her answer, Terelle responded, "That would be much appreciated."

"I'll write you that note right now."

Several minutes later, the woman returned with a note.

"This should help you as much as anything. If you go out the doorway and turn left, it will be the ninth place on the right-hand side. His name is Darmer. He likes to call himself Darmer the Armorer, but he deals in all sorts of goods."

"I've been meaning to ask," Terelle stated, "but what name do you go by?"

Touched that Terelle wanted to know the wench's name, she smiled and answered, "Sarah...they call me Sarah."

"Okay Sarah, we will return shortly."

The newly formed party picked up all the extra gear, and then tied a rope around the prisoner that was then tethered around Splats' waist. Terelle led the way to the local merchant.

When they came upon the proper building, they could see the mercantile sign hanging above the door. As with most doors, this door wasn't large enough to accommodate Splat.

"Splat," Terelle reasoned, "why don't you stay out here and watch our prisoner?"

"Okay, him not go anywhere," Splat replied, and then set down an armload of loot before sitting against the side of the building.

Dain, Dinly, and Trina followed Terelle into the store. From the outside they could see that the business was quite large for a mercantile and figured Darner must be doing very well for himself. As the four of them entered, they could see that the man had an extensive inventory of nearly anything one could ask for.

The man behind the counter was large, for a human, and acted well-mannered as they approached.

"Hello folks! What can I do for ya?"

"Are you Darmer the Armorer?" Terelle asked.

"No Ma'am, he's in the back. Is there something I can help you with?"

"I have a note for him. Would you please ask him to come to the front?" Terelle smiled pleasantly.

A door to the back opened.

"No need for that Miss. I heard you asking for me. Now what's this about a note?"

Darmer wasn't near the size of the man behind the counter, and he had a balding head and spectacles; he looked like a real bookworm.

Terelle handed over the letter and let him have a chance to read it. His surprise over what the note contained was evident on his face.

"Well, I'll be damned! My cousin at the tavern sent you to me and it says here that you all killed that creep Marty and four of his men. Too bad you didn't get the rest of them!"

"Oh, we have one of them outside. How many men did he have?" Terelle inquired knowing the information would be very useful during the next day or two.

"Not considering the one you have, there are still five more that I know of," Darmer informed the party.

"Well, we plan to get outfitted properly and then see

what we can do about the rest of them."

"I see, Darmer said as he looked over the group's loot. "It looks as if you have some extra gear. Are you trying to trade that for what you need?"

"To some extent, yes. Two of us are ready to go, but these three here," she waved her hand to include her three new companions, "need some things."

Darmer figured that the party had the other party member with the prisoner, so he chose not to ask where that person was.

"How much of that gear are you wanting to get rid of?" The merchant started calculating things in his head.

Trina spoke up, holding two items up in her left hand.

"I want this sword and this dagger, but nothing else from this mess."

"She also needs travel clothes, a cloak, a pair of high, soft boots in her size and some other items," Terelle stated. "The Dwarf will need a few minor items, and the Halfling will need close to a full loadout, if my guess is correct."

"Are you looking for any armor at all?" Darmer asked. "I have some studded leather that would fit the Halfling, and nearly any kind to fit Miss Robes there."

"Let's try some chainmail on her and see what she thinks, and the studded leather sounds like a good start for Dinly."

Darmer went into the back and brought out several items in short order.

"I'll be honest with you. I only have one lady's blouse that will fit you," he spoke to Trina. "If you want more, there is a seamstress up the road a few doors that can stitch you up some pretty quick."

"Thank you," Trina responded.

"I also have zero braziers right now, and my supply of candles is quite low. I have some things coming in next week, but I realize that that might be too late."

"I think we will do just fine for today," Terelle notified the man. She then gathered some items that were out front before asking, "Do you have a short sword with scabbard?"

"Dozens," the merchant answered.

"I would like to see them so I can pick one."

"Very well. I have them laid out in the back. You can follow me."

Leaving the others in the front, she walked through the door with the merchant. The whole back room was filled with all sorts of weapons and armor, along with various other goods, mostly in bulk. She let her eyes land on a table that had short swords spread out, and she took her time looking at each one. After notifying the merchant of her desire to do so and getting his permission she cast a minor spell that revealed that none of the swords had any curses on them. With an "All Clear" result, she then proceeded to pick up each weapon in turn and check it for sharpness, strength, and durability. It didn't take her long to choose a few that met her requirements. Terelle asked if she could check the few that she liked for magic.

"Sure can, as long as you are casting toward the table. But I can save you the spell if you like. These two have magical properties, and this third one here was finely crafted by a master armorer."

"Thank you."

She then cast her spell only to find that the merchant was telling the truth. One can never be too certain with someone you don't know and trust when it comes to such matters. She chose the magic weapon that also had a steel scabbard.

"I see you have abilities. This one is expensive...I hope you have more than just items to pay for it," he smiled as he spoke.

"I have some, and I know what fair market price is for it. What are you asking?"

He paused for a moment in a moment of reflection.

"Equivalent of thirteen hundred and twenty," Darmer announced.

"That's about ten percent over market."

"Yes, but the scabbard is enchanted as well. It's an

Ever-sharp scabbard and worth the extra cost."

"Do you take gems?"

"Only after they are verified by a friend of mine. He is only next door and we can easily go there now."

Terelle and Darmer walked back out to the store area and she noticed that nobody had tried on any of the gear set out for them.

"Trina...Dinly, please try on the clothes and armor. We will be back in a few minutes."

"Do you expect us to change right here?" Trina asked.

"I have a dressing room around the corner to your left that you can use," Darmer spoke to the women.

"Okay, thank you" Dinly acknowledge and grabbed her things.

Terelle and the merchant walked outside and Darmer nearly lost his composure. Terelle noticed and made introductions between the merchant and Splat. Darmer also noticed the prisoner and smirked at the man as he and Terelle left to go next door.

Minutes passed as the women tried on the clothes and armor set out for them. As Trina was pulling on the chain shirt, Terelle and Darmer walked back in.

Seeing that Dinly was now wearing the armor, Terelle stopped to look it over.

"How does it feel?"

"Like I'm a bit more protected than before, and it's loose enough in the areas it needs to be...I like it."

"Is Trina in the dressing room?"

"I'm on my way out," Trina called as she turned the corner with the travel clothes and the chainmail on.

"What do you think?" Terelle asked.

"It'll take some getting used to, but I'd rather have the protection."

"Let's get Trina some boots if you have any," she directed to Darmer.

The merchant asked Trina to stand with one bare foot in a measuring device.

"Good...I have a few pairs of boots in your size. Let's try them on, shall we?"

The merchant came back with four pair of solid boots and Trina tried them on.

"These feel a bit big. Are you sure they're the right size?" Trina asked after trying on all four pair.

"Yes," Darmer explained, "but I've noticed that sometimes a woman's feet are slightly smaller than the boots allow for. Shy of having some made, the best idea I have is to use stockings on your feet. Let me get some."

The merchant brought a pair of thick wool stockings and had her put them on, then the boots.

Relieved, Trina commented, "Wow! That is so much

better."

She then tried on the rest of the boots, finding one pair that fit very well. She asked Terelle if she could get extra stockings and ended up with four pair.

Once finished with things out front, Terelle and Darmer went into the back room again and exchanged two Rubies for the short sword and scabbard.

Coming back out and handing the short sword and dagger to Dinly, Terelle asked if there was anything else that anyone needed that they couldn't find.

Dinly spoke up, "I could use some lock picks and butcher's gloves if there are any."

"Yes, I have those items. I'll be right back," Darmer was quick to respond.

The merchant was back in a minute holding a box of picks and three sizes of dense metallic gloves.

Dinly quickly found the size of gloves she wanted, and then sorted through the picks. She wished she could take all of them but kept the number down to twenty of the lock picks she thought would work the best for most occasions.

"Okay Darmer, how much do we get from the exchange?" Terelle asked.

"Ha, now that's funny," the man smiled. "What with the picks, food, skins, bracers, armor, clothes, shields, cloaks, and everything else...I'd be hard pressed to let you out the door without charging at least 20 gold over the credit for what you brought."

"Come now!" Terelle spoke up louder, "With all of the gear we brought in, you could nearly outfit six men. We should have at least 10 silver coming back to us."

"Hogwash! If I lose money on every transaction, how am I supposed to pay the help, let alone buy food to eat?" the merchant complained.

This was an exercise in how bartering works. It doesn't matter if you are getting a good deal, you must still go high, while the other person goes low. Then you go back and forth until both parties agree on something in the middle.

"You should try eating less, or at least pick less expensive food, or you will never break even," Terelle retorted. "I'll tell you what, we can settle on not having to pay anything, or maybe pay this guard here a few silver for having to put up with the wages I'm sure you are not setting high enough."

"Bah!" Darmer exclaimed, "He costs too much already, and I already have someone make my food from the least expensive ingredients...I'll take fifteen gold and let you give this poor man ten silver for his help."

"Perhaps you should cook your own food if it's costing too much to have someone else cook it. And I don't recall this man helping all that much...definitely not ten silver worth. I'll give you two gold and five silver," Terelle countered

"You'd have me pay this man coppers to help fend off ruffians and watch me eat bread alone!" Darmer cried. "Make it eleven gold and fifteen silver, and just maybe I can afford a bone to add to my boiling water. You haggle like no woman I've ever had to deal with before, wanting me to starve to death!"

After a few more rounds of this, they came to agree on the party paying six gold and seven silver, plus the equipment the party got from the bandits that day. The gems for the short sword and scabbard were a separate transaction involving the same process of haggling.

Once the bill was paid, the companions thanked the merchant and went back to the tavern. There was already a man at the doorway taking measurements as they arrived. He looked at Splat and shook his head. He started taking measurements again, but from far to the side, leaving plenty of room for Splat to get through.

Terelle walked up to Sarah, who was trying to ignore a man grabbing her rear end and asked her to come talk in private.

"Hey lady, I was ordering some food!" the man grumbled.

"No, you were grabbing her butt," Terelle replied.

"Well, you don't have to get jealous. I have another hand for you, too," he said with a smile that showed a mouth with half a set of teeth that looked like they also needed pulling.

"You won't if I cut it off now, would you?" she asked.

The man noticed Splat and the others with her and decided to shut his mouth, not wanting to push his luck any further.

Terelle and Sarah walked to a dark, empty area and Terelle handed her something.

"Your cousin didn't take advantage of us too much. I thank you."

Sarah looked at the coins in her hand and nearly fainted.

"I, I don't know what to say! Thank you...thank you so very much!"

Sarah had five gold and five silver in her hand. She had never had as much as one gold of her own in her whole life.

"Don't sweat it. Another merchant would have charged us four or five times that much," Terelle told her.

Terelle smiled inside. Except for the short sword, she had broken even with the majority of the money they had taken from the bandits they had fought this day. She and Splat still had plenty of money from their adventures, and a whole lot more than they had spent today, even after factoring in the gems used to buy the short sword.

3

After midnight, the companions decided it was time to start looking for the other bandits from the gang of thieves they had started getting rid of earlier in the day.

"Okay mister, it's time to see if you want to live or die," Terelle told their prisoner. "Start leading the way. Oh...and if you lead us into a trap, you will not only die, but you will die a very painful and slow death."

Dain only vaguely remembered the walk that evening. He was very happy to have a few of the smaller items he had not thought of before. Now he had a full kit, some friends he felt he could rely upon, and his first adventure out of town. It was a good thing the prisoner wanted to live, because Dain wasn't paying proper attention.

He wasn't alone. Trina was trying to get used to wearing breeches and blouse, instead of her billowing robes. Added to that, she was having difficulty adjusting to the weight of the chain mail, a full pack, and a sword in a scabbard on the belt around her waist. She was also deep in thought, second-guessing her actions. *What am I doing? I don't even know how to use a sword.* But she had really liked the way it felt in her hand, so she decided to keep it.

Dinly was trying to pay attention. She was used to

having to watch everything and everybody she came near. She now had a full belly, a real weapon, and oh so many things that would be helpful in keeping her alive. She was grateful enough to these fine people that she even figured she owed them her allegiance, at least for a while anyways. She would have to see how things went before committing to anything long term.

"We are getting close," the prisoner whispered to Terelle.

"Okay," she whispered back, and then put a hand up to stop the others.

Splat stopped, and the other three companions, coming up behind him, clumsily bumped into the person in front of them producing a series of clunks and rattles from the collision of metal and leather. It would have been comical if the situation weren't so serious.

Terelle gathered them all in a circle and admonished the newcomers.

"If you can't be quiet and pay attention you will get us all killed.!"

Though she whispered, she came through loud and clear, noticing three very solemn faces.

"Now..." she looked at the prisoner, "Where is this place and what is the layout?"

"There's an old abandoned farmhouse over there," he

pointed. "And there is a large barn across from it to our right. There are some smaller things like a pig pen and chicken coop, but the house and barn are the only places to worry about...except maybe the outhouse, which is on the right of the barn as one looks at it. There will be at least one guard in the barn with the girls, and one in the house watching toward our direction. We are about half a mile out, so there is plenty of room to flank the buildings without being seen. This time of night, at least two should be sleeping. I say should, because the rest of us never came back and they might be getting restless about our absence."

Terelle listened to him. She didn't just hear him relay the very detailed description of the farm, she really listened to him and was impressed.

"You sound well educated for a common bandit."

"Hard times make hard people. I wasn't always like this, but it's too late for me now," he looked down at the ground as he spoke. "I will likely die tonight, even though I'm leading you honestly."

"If you do live, you should try starting over somewhere far from here and do something good with your life," Terelle whispered.

Whispering from a half mile may seem a bit out of sorts, but there are beings that are capable of hearing from farther away than that. If the prisoner was whispering, she figured it a good idea to continue doing so.

"If I'm given the chance, I most certainly will give it a try," he responded.

"Let's get back to the task at hand," Terelle refocused and then again glanced toward the prisoner. "I have to ask. Is there anyone there that you are going to miss?"

"One of them owes me a small amount of money, but otherwise," he shook his head, "no."

"Okay then...Splat and I will take the farmhouse. Dain and Dinly, you two have the barn."

"What about me?" Trina asked.

"Somebody has to watch..." Terelle stopped and looked toward the prisoner with sudden realization. "Hell, I've never even asked your name."

"Jacob."

"Jacob what?" Terelle inquired.

Jacob blushed, barely visible in the dark, but one could hear the hesitation.

"Jacob Cobblestone."

There were a couple of hushed snickers from Splat and Trina.

"Okay," Dain couldn't resist, "I just got to know how you got that name?"

"I was found outside of a home in a village where you get a surname based on something about you if you don't have a family name. My crib was on the cobblestones of the walkway to the home I was taken into for my rearing."

"Oh! With my people, being named for any stone is something to be proud of, and cobblestones are a very important item to make roads with. You should be proud of your name," Dain remarked. "I figure you need to find a way to be proud of yourself first, and that may take a very long time."

Dain looked to Terelle, "Let's go, shall we?"

The companions swung around to one side just like Jacob had suggested. When they got within a couple of hundred yards, they tied Jacob to a tree so he couldn't escape. The four assigned to take out the guards then proceeded forward with caution until they were less than fifty yards away. Terelle had them stop, using hand signals to do so, and verified that all were paying close attention.

Using her Infravision she was able to detect no significant heat signature coming from the outhouse. With fires in the house and barn, it was too difficult to really determine any detail as to how many were in each building. She could, however, tell that nobody was outside, unless they were covering their heat signature somehow.

She motioned for them to split up and move forward, carefully, and in an around about way so as not to be seen.

Dinly led the way in the direction to the barn. She was

starting to notice that, compared to her light footsteps, Dain sounded like a herd of elephants moving along. It was unfortunate that she hadn't noticed this earlier when she had time to stop and secure some of his noisy gear. The others wouldn't be stopping, so she had to hope for the best.

Terelle had always appreciated how softly Splat could walk, considering his size. He would never sneak up on an Elf, but he could usually sneak up on any human if he wanted to. Her main worry was if Splat could fit through the farmhouse door or not. It was usually not. This meant he would have to watch the back door of the house, if there was one, and that she might have to clear the house by herself. This was the main reason she took him with her. The other two could fight together.

As they approached the house, she had Splat stop and wait while she snuck around the back. She traversed the ground all around the house, ducking under the two windows, and found no other doors.

Even in the dimness of night, Splat could see enough for her to signal for him to stay by the door and take out anyone who tries to leave. The darn door was barely large enough to comfortably let in a human, such was her luck.

She approached the door, lightly gripped the handle, and discovered that it was locked. *Great, so much for being quiet,* she thought. Terelle waved Splat closer, and they waited until they heard noises from the barn. Terelle stood at one side of the door and Splat at the other. With Splat's last step, the boards underneath him creaked.

Dinly made her way to the barn door and tested it. *Locked!*, she thought. *I don't have time for this.* She slipped a hand into an inner pocket within her new cloak and pulled out a pick she hoped would work on this lock. After several seconds, she was rewarded with a satisfying soft click, meaning she had accessed the tumbler node. She then tried turning it clockwise. *No, that way doesn't work.* She tried counterclockwise, being careful not to lose her placing, for locks can be finicky when trying both directions.

She was rewarded with the lock mechanism turning a full quarter circle, unlocking the door. This took nearly a full minute. She'd have to practice more before another adventure.

Dain was standing behind her and off to one side, waiting impatiently. *Finally!* he thought as she was able to unlock the door. As she did so, the knob turned, the door opened, and a gruff looking bandit spoke.

"Well, what have we here?"

The bandit then noticed Dain as Dain swung his axe.

Surprised, the man reacted fast. It was almost fast

enough...ALMOST. Killing another is a gruesome thing, and this was so much more so than usual. Dain had tried an overhead swing to split the man in half, but the man backed up to where Dain's axe only took off the man's face from the eyebrows forward. The man fell backwards and landed hard. Dain struggled to pull his axe from the wooden floor while another man called out.

"Red, what's going on…"

Dinly charged in with her short sword drawn and met the naked man as he was reaching for a broadsword. She plunged her sword into his belly at an angle that would place the blade's end into his chest. It would have worked perfectly if she had used her strength properly.

With the short sword stuck in his gut, the bandit backhanded the little Halfling, sending her several feet away. Grasping his sword hilt with both hands, he stumbled toward her to make sure she would never injure anyone again.

Dain was faster. Having no luck pulling his axe out in time, he closed in on the man who could only see Dinly. Dain had his dagger and a full head of steam as he reached up and slammed the dagger down along the man's spine from behind.

Seemingly possessing superhuman powers, the man stopped, half turned toward the Dwarf, and started to bring his sword around. But that was all. He collapsed like a puppet with its strings cut all at once.

Dain and Dinly quickly looked around to see if there were anyone else that wanted to kill them. The only other people they saw were several young females all tied up in various stages of undress, one laying on the floor with only a bit of straw under her, right where the naked man had come up from.

The faceless man wasn't quite out of this yet. He groaned an indistinct sound that emanated from the gaping, bloody hole where his mouth should have been, as he started to get up. Dinly noticed him and stepped over to the dead man and started pulling out her short sword.

Dain noticed what she was doing and the frantic way she was doing it, so he turned to see the gruesome face approaching. He had just missed taking away the man's eyes and opening the skull. The man would die soon, but not soon enough. Dain ran at the man at full speed, using a flying shoulder tackle to slow the man down.

It had the desired effect, knocking the man back down and giving Dinly the time she needed to retrieve her weapon, come over, and give the man the coup de grass.

****

Terelle didn't know what to expect, but hearing a man ask "Well, what do we have here?" wasn't it. She contemplated going over to the barn to help when she heard the door unlock in front of her.

The man tried to rush out to the aid of his buddies when Terelle stuck her sword through his ribcage. In one well-placed lunge, she had finished the man off. To his demise, the man had mistakenly figured that Terelle was one of the females sent to give him a good time and had ignored her as a threat. By the time he registered in his head that she was armed, it was too late.

She and Splat could hear more noise inside the house. Terelle dragged the body away from the doorway as another man came running out. He wasn't very quiet about it and Splat's timing was spot-on.

The man took the full force of the Half-Giant's swing with the pointed maul, and the damage was devastating. With his entire rib cage crushed inward, the man flew backward into the house. He was dead before Splat's weapon had stopped forward momentum.

In a hunched over half-run, Terelle rushed into the house and slid left, easily seeing the last man in the house, obviously in shock, standing at an interior doorway. She didn't hesitate, took two steps forward, and cut the man's head off. He hadn't even moved as his body crumpled to the floor.

She quickly looked for any others, but only found a fire burning in the fireplace. She headed back out to rally with Splat and check on the others.

Dain asked Dinly to untie the girls while he retrieved his axe. He started to walk outside as Terelle and Splat showed up.

Splat looked at the axe embedded in the floor and noted the lack of much blood.

"Why not use weapon?"

"I got it stuck in the wood...must have swung it too hard," Dain explained as he struggled trying to pull it out.

"Let me try," Splat announced.

Splat first tried, unsuccessfully with one hand and said with surprise in his deep voice, "Hmmm, stuck!"

Then he set down his maul and used the massive strength of both arms, which achieved the desired result when it finally came free.

"Axe was real stuck!" the half-Giant stated as he handed it back to Dain.

Terelle spoke next, "I take it by the casual way you walked to the doorway that you have things under control in there."

"Yes," Dain answered.

"And that you weren't worried about anyone getting

through us?"

Dain assessed the question and realized his carelessness, stating, "Oh, sorry. I think I need some training if I'm going to stay alive. I've been doing really poorly today."

"Yes, we will be talking a bit about that."

Terelle and Splat followed Dain into the barn. At least the main barn doors were large enough to accommodate Splat's immense frame. Dain walked over to the interior latch for the doors and unlatched them, letting Splat inside.

After seeing the rescued girls that Dinly was untying, Terelle started to help comfort them.

"Splat, go get Trina and Jacob, would you?"

A few minutes later, Splat returned with Trina and the prisoner, Jacob. One of the closest girls jumped up at the sight of Jacob and ran straight to him, threw her arms around him, and started crying.

Terelle walked over and asked, "What's going on here? I thought he and the others were raping you."

The girl, Jessica was her name, then told her story.

"They did, repeatedly, but not him. Oh, he told us one night that he would have to do so to one of us, every so often, or the others would think he was a spy, but overall he helped us. He would bring us extra food and water when no one was watching, and would bring us soap, water, and a dishrag so we could clean up...um...you know...when he had night watch. I took him when he was forced into it by the others, and he was never rough like they were. Jacob made things just bearable in an otherwise unbearable situation. Heck, he even let us use blankets when he was on watch. None of the others would."

"It sounds like you just might make a life for yourself after all, Jacob," Terelle advised as she looked him in the eyes, hard.

"Thank you, but I still have a lot to make up for," Jacob sheepishly said as he looked at the ground.

"Well, at least all you girls can go home in a few hours," Terelle said.

Jessica, with tears in her eyes looked straight at Terelle and explained, "Not all of us can. The youngest girl, Isabelle, and I have no place to go."

"Let me think on it some," Terelle told the young lady.

As dawn approached, Trina and Dinly looked in the kitchen of the house and found some cooking utensils and dishes. Looking in the larder, they found it was quite full and decided to make everyone some breakfast. Dain had already cleared the bodies from the house, and Splat did the same in the barn. They also piled anything useful next to a wagon that was in the open bay of the barn.

Terelle had just finished feeding the team of horses that were behind the barn in a fenced field when the food was ready.

Everyone, except Jacob, sat near the fireplace in the barn to eat. Jacob was offered food but said he would only eat if there was anything left after everyone else was done.

"Jacob," Terelle started talking after eating most of her hard sausage, eggs and fried biscuits. "I've been talking to the other girls and thinking. Your team of bandits stole an awful lot of supplies and money. We are going to take some of it back to give to the rightful owners. Another portion will be given to each of these young ladies for the torture they've endured, but I'm also going to give you just a small amount to get you started somewhere. All of these ladies have agreed that you should be given the chance to live, and they have agreed that you should be given enough supplies to get you there. How do you feel about that?"

Jacob sat up a bit straighter and announced with hope in his voice, "That is more than I could have ever dreamed for. I will take whatever it is and move far away from here...try to start over, the right way this time."

"Good, that's what I wanted to hear."

"Miss Terelle?" Jessica asked. "Is it okay if Isabell and I go with him? We've already talked it over between us."

"Isabell is the young girl who also has no more

family?"

"Yes, she is."

"I see no reason to keep you from living the life you want. Huh, it might even keep Jacob out of trouble if he must take care of others who rely upon him. Done deal."

"Oh, thank you, Miss Terelle," Jessica gushed as a flood of relief spread across her face.

"No need to thank me. Like I said, it's your choice."

Terelle then started in on the next point of business.

"Okay, there are just over 1200 gold, 3600 silver, 900 mixed smelt rounds, and 18,000 copper rounds. This is a huge amount of coin, and most is going back to the town, but each girl will get 50 gold rounds and 200 silver rounds each. Jacob, you will get the remaining small amounts of each coin, which is 7 gold, 49 silver, 16 mixed smelt, and 131 copper rounds. The three of you will get the draft horses and wagon after we deliver the girls and most of the money to the townsfolk. Jacob, you will also get weapons and clothing of your own, and you and the two girls will get any supplies we don't take back to town or keep for ourselves. All other items and money found on the bodies has been piled up and is ours for our efforts. We will start by loading up the wagon with a large part of the supplies stored here. Then, we'll load up the money after everyone gets their part, and then we will get to moving toward town.

Jacob, you get to help Dain load the supplies into the wagon. Splat, you have watch. Ladies, let's get things organized, cleaned, and the money separated. Jacob, you will be allowed to stay untied, but don't make us hunt you down...you won't get a third chance."

Terelle and Trina had to donate whatever extra clothing they had, but it wasn't enough. Two of the girls had to fashion sheets into robes just to cover themselves. The three girls in the worst shape would ride in the wagon next to Terelle. Everyone else would have to walk, except for Jessica and Dinly who would ride on the only extra horse.

4

The now enlarged group came within sight of Windy Dale. Within minutes, and still just on the edge of town, a crowd was gathering.

It wasn't long before a man in the crowd excitedly called out, "Shelly, Shelly, is that you?"

"Hi dad!" a girl on the wagon answered.

The man ran up to the slowly moving wagon and lifted his daughter out. He held onto her in a big hug like she had been gone forever, and as far as he was concerned, she very well could have been.

"Dad, we need to follow the wagon," the girl told her father.

"Okay honey, if you say so."

He carried his fifteen-year-old another block and a half until the wagon stopped in front of Longtree Tavern.

News spread quickly that the companions had not only come back but were bringing several of the town's girls with them. They were being hailed as heroes, all except Jacob, that is. There were many that were calling for a hanging regarding Jacob, and who could blame them? None of the townsfolk knew of the good he tried to do in a bad situation, or of the deal given to him by the companions.

The Mayor of the town showed up and she had a man at her side. She came up to the wagon, where three of the girls now had family members there to embrace them and talked briefly with Terelle about the goings on that led to this moment. She also recognized Jacob and mentioned a hanging.

Terelle stood atop the wagon and shouted, "People, Mayor Monica...there will be no hanging of this man. To try it would mean having to kill us as well."

"That could be arranged!" a man yelled from the back.

Terelle was quick to notice the boisterous man and those gathered around him and admonished, "That would be a big mistake sir! But if you think you should try to kill those who did what you and your friends failed to do, then by all means, come and try! If you good folks between us would be so kind as to step aside and let this man and his buddies' approach, we can get this over with."

She watched as a pathway parted amongst much murmuring, and yet, the man and his friends did not come forward.

"That's what I thought! This town could have come together and taken out the threat of the robber gang, but it didn't. And now! Now that the gang is gone, you have someone with a voice...a voice, but no balls! We've vanquished your foes, brought back your girls, and a large sum of your town's money and supplies. We did this for no reward...just trying to make this a better place to come and rest after whatever trials are before us...and we get somebody telling us he can get us killed. Killed for what?"

Incensed, she was still yelling at the townsfolk.

"Killed because we gave our word to a man that likely saved your girls' lives? We have honor and we don't see enough of that here. If we can buy a few horses that will be enough for us. If not, we can make do without them. Either way, we will be leaving here shortly, and we will find another town for our base."

She lowered her voice to normal and continued, "Now Mayor, I assume you have people to help unload our wagon if you want what we brought you."

It took nearly half an hour to complete the transactions in town. Terelle and Trina led four horses from a couple of blocks away back to the now empty wagon. Terelle noticed the loud-mouthed man and three of his friends following them, staying half a block away.

Once back at the wagon, she quickly notified the others of what she saw. Splat was always very protective of Terelle, and this time was no different. He picked up his maul, ready to fight, when the men came to the nearby corner with their hands on hilts.

Splat didn't even warn anyone, he just charged into the

men and started swinging his weapon. The giant wrecking ball named Splat crushed two of the men before the other two could even lift their swords to fight back. The rest of the battle took less than thirty seconds, the giant giving no quarter. It didn't end well for the men.

"You got a nick on your left arm," Terelle notified her faithful friend.

"One of them good with sword...not good no more."

Trina came up to help, asking. "Do you think it was smart to just attack like that?"

She started to bandage Splat's arm, noticing that the wound was almost non-existent and appeared to be healing right in front of her eyes.

"If not now, then they come when we sleep and try," Splat said and then pointed at Terelle. "It's one thing she teach me about others."

The Mayor and the man with her earlier walked up.

"Are you sure you won't base yourselves out of our town?" the Mayor asked.

Terelle pointed to the bodies to emphasize her point, saying, "With your residents acting like that toward us? No thank you!"

"Those men aren't our residents...they came in late last night. I had it checked out," the Mayor stated.

"Oh good! Then we lay claim to any supplies they

brought with them."

"They stabled horses across the street from where you bought your horses and were staying at the Inn right there," the Mayor pointed to the Dragon Scale Inn.

"Thank you, we will think about any offers you may have to keep us in this area."

Terelle 's mind was working at ideas.

"We do get a lot of traffic through here, and we could use some help from time to time. I could make it where any trade you do with the townsfolk would be tax exempt in return for that help," the Mayor practically begged.

"So, we would be LOW paid mercenaries for the town?" Terelle asked.

"We are a fairly poor town. Maybe there is something else you want?"

"There is an old abandoned farm where we found the girls. If you give us clear deed to that and we keep all goods and livestock from any combatants we get rid of for the town, we would be willing to help the town when we can. We might be gone for months at a time. There's no way to tell when we'd be here, but we could help when needed whenever we are here. Oh, and you would need to inform your people as to why we would stay. If those terms are okay with you, then I think I could get the others to go along with it."

"What about the taxes?" the Mayor questioned.

"We will pay taxes like anyone else. Just make sure you don't try to make ours higher than the other residents, or you may not like the outcome."

"That much I can do. Talk it over and let me know if you accept. I'll have my scribe write it up."

Terelle gathered everyone at the wagon and informed Dain and Dinly of the conversation with the Mayor, as Splat and Trina had already heard it. All agreed to the terms, although Dain had a question.

"What are we going to do with a farm?" Dain asked.

"It occurred to me after learning that the idiots weren't from here and that we just gained some more livestock, that Sarah the server wench and her son, and maybe even the other serving wench, might be better off if they don't have to pay for housing. With a couple of horses, they could ride to and from work. This would give us a real base of operations, and if things went right, they could start working for us as caretakers instead."

"Have you thought to ask them first?" Dinly asked, stretching to her full height of nearly three and a half feet, to be seen.

"No, not yet. I was heading in right now to see if they are even there," Terelle informed the Halfling. "Splat, why don't you finish stripping the bodies of anything useful?"

They had already grabbed most of the weapons from the four dead men before the Mayor had walked up.

"Okay, got it," Splat answered.

"Trina, can you watch Splats back?" asked Terelle.

"Sure!"

"Dinly and Dain, please keep an eye on the horses and wagon, will you?"

"Sure thing!" Dinly answered for both of them.

Terelle walked into the tavern. Sarah was there with another serving wench, but not the one she had seen before. She waited patiently for a couple of minutes until Sarah was available and then asked for a few minutes of Sarah's time. Sarah asked the other wench to cover for her for a few minutes before going to a small table near the back, away from most of the patrons, to talk with Terelle.

"I have a few minutes. What did you want to talk about?" Sarah asked.

"Sarah, I have an opportunity for you and your son. It might be for the other ladies that work here as well."

"I'm listening."

"We are acquiring a farm outside of town. It is only a start to what we want to do, but a start it is," Terelle began and then paused for a second before going on, hoping she wasn't overthinking things. "Problem is, we won't be there much, and we don't want to leave it abandoned like it is. We were wondering if you, and maybe one or more of your co-workers, might want to live there, instead of here in town.”

“How far out of town is it?”

“A few miles, but we would also leave a couple of horses for you, so you can travel back and forth.”

“What will it cost me?”

“Only what you put into it, along with feed and the such for the horses. The house will be yours and any others who come along. We will use the barn loft until we have another home built for us on the property.”

“You mean we will stay for free?”

“As free as you want to make it,” Terelle answered.

“What’s the catch?” Sarah skeptically asked.

“Only one slight catch.”

“Aha! I knew it!”

Terelle quickly eased Sarah’s worries by explaining the few basic requirements that the group would ask of her and her friends.

“We only ask you and any others to make us a meal or two and take care of our livestock for a day when we first get back from being out. Oh, and that you take care of the place on your own. If it’s going to be your home, then you don’t want to just let it fall down around you.”

“That’s it?” Sarah’s disbelief showed.

“That’s it,” Terelle confirmed.

"When do you need to know?"

"Within a couple of days would be nice."

Terelle gave Sarah directions to the farm so she and her friends could look it over and better determine if it was truly a good deal.

"I'll let you know by the night of the day after tomorrow after I finish my shift, if that's soon enough."

"That will work just fine, Sarah."

"We did pretty good," Dain told Terelle when she came out of the tavern. "They had four riding horses and two work horses for carrying their extra equipment. They also had a fair amount of money on them and we haven't even looked into their room yet."

"Then maybe we should go check that out right now," Terelle stated. "Dain, you and I will go. You three stay here until we get back, will ya?"

The others were in agreement.

A few minutes later, Terelle and Dain rejoined their companions.

They were both smiling as Terelle announced, "We need to take the wagon to the Inn...we aren't pack horses."

The contents of the room contained enough weapons and armor to outfit at least seven men at arms. At first, everyone thought they were going to sell these items and split the money. But Terelle had something else in mind.

"No, we are going to hold onto them for future use. That way we don't lose the difference between selling at ten percent or more less than the actual value and buying at ten percent or more above actual value later."

"Why would we do that?" Dain asked.

Making sure nobody could hear her idea except her companions, Terelle laid out a series of thoughts. The companions, except Splat, all smiled at the ideas and started thinking about the implications of what she said.

****

The group of adventurers were relaxing around a campfire just outside the barn at the farm when Sarah, her son, two tavern wenches, and a man showed up.

Sarah spoke first.

"After talking it over, the five of us would like to take you up on your offer, if it is still available."

"Yes, it is," Terelle answered. "Though I have to say that I didn't know a man was invited."

"He is married to Kindra here, and he is good at carpentry. He could help with the repairs around here and he would eventually add extra sleeping quarters for us, so we aren't in each other's way."

"Don't misunderstand," Terelle smiled, "I'm actually glad that there will be a man here. I was worried about only women and children living out here at the farm. It will be good to have the five of you here. How soon can you move in?"

Sarah continued to be the spokesperson for the newcomers.

"We all have rental agreements, except for Deidra here, and will not be able to leave our commitments until the week is over. However, we all wanted to see the place and find out how much work needed to be done and how long that work would take to accomplish. Deidra has two days off now and can start getting things ready sometime tomorrow if she could get use of your horses and wagon. What say you?"

"This is possible," Terelle confirmed. The house is unlocked, you may go in and see it for yourself. We will just stay here and let you be."

After the townsfolk walked over to the house, Terelle spoke to the others at the fire pit.

"I will let Jacob, Jessica, and Isabelle know once they wake up tomorrow that they will have to stick around for a few more days. We could get another wagon, but I don't see a need for that expense right now."

Once Terelle finished her statement, Dinly excused herself to go quietly to the barn loft to think.

I can't believe my luck. I have clothes being made for me, boots being made to fit my feet, a full belly on a regular basis without fish. I have armor, weapons, food in my pack and a full purse. If only that storekeeper could see me now. In fact, I think I will see about us heading that direction and pay a visit to not only the storekeeper, but the sheriff too. She continued to think of many things for several more minutes as she became drowsy. The last thing she recalled thinking before she faded off to sleep was *But by far...the most exciting prospect is that bunch of ideas in Terelle's head.*

"Well, what do you think?" Terelle asked Sarah.

"It's a bit hard to tell all the details by torchlight, and it's a bit small for us all, but we can make it work. With the money we will all save we can afford the materials for Sid to build another home in not much time. Once that is done, we will start to actually upgrade our lives, thanks to you all and your generosity."

"Since you are here, I need to tell you all something. We will be storing some supplies of various kinds in the loft above the barn. We expect them to still be there each time we come back. Part of the supplies are weapons and armor. Do any of you have any experience with either?"

Sid spoke up, "I can handle a bow pretty well and have a basic knowledge of sword tactics, but that is it."

"Good, then we will supply you with those and a bit of leather armor from the supplies. Those items are still ours, but you should have use of them."

Terelle then mentioned for the others to join the companions around the fire and all, but the young boy, talked for a couple of hours, getting to know each other.

It was five days later when Jacob, Jessica, and Isabelle were finally able to load up their belongings and what supplies they were allotted into the wagon and headed for parts unknown.

With two horses gone and two more staying at the farm, the companions still had four riding horses and the two work horses to carry their supplies. The companions found it necessary to go back into town for their own needs.

First on their list was to pick up the clothing and boots that had been ordered, then to Sarah's cousin's store to buy some small items they had missed. They also picked up some extra rations and feed for their first real journey together. As they were coming out of Darmer's place, the Mayor walked up to them.

"I see you are heading out."

"Yes, and thank you for drafting the deed and

agreement so fast for us," Terelle spoke for the group as she had the best way with words in this kind of situation and was the leader of the group.

"When I agreed to this, I didn't know that the place came with so much land. 640 acres is a lot to contend with. Are you sure you don't want something smaller?" the Mayor inquired.

"No, we're happy with what we have," Terelle replied.

"Very well then. Are you going to be gone long?" the Mayor asked.

"We have no idea. It's kind of the nature of it. We know which direction we are going, but we don't have any particular destination in mind. I'm pretty sure we won't be gone long, but you just never know."

5

"Are you sure that this should be our first real outing?" Dinly asked.

She had made the mistake of talking to the others about the idea of going to her hometown hamlet of Valley's Edge and clearing up any debts she still had.

Dain answered her, "Look little filly...if we are to be a solid company, we need to first clear up any messes we have left behind."

"I have to agree with Dain," Terelle added. "You now have the ability to clear any transgressions you may have had. We need to clear your name, so we aren't looking over our shoulders because of it. Besides, you did say it wasn't very far from here."

"That's true, but I don't want to be a burden to the rest of you. I could just take care of this while you guys do something more important."

Dinly looked for the reactions of her new friends.

"Nonsense!" Trina added. "We are a team now. What kind of team would we be if we let you do this alone?"

"Besides," Terelle interjected, "if there is a problem that is too big to handle on your own, we will have your back."

"Yeah, me splat em for you too, little one!" Splat said firmly.

Dain waited a few seconds before coming out with his own thoughts.

"I was wondering...with four of us on horses, how will the big guy here keep up with us, especially if we have to move quickly?"

Though expecting Terelle to answer, it was Splat himself who replied, "Easy, me fly!"

That was it. Answered simply and still not making any sense at all to the Dwarf.

"How would you do that?" Dain asked.

"If need, you will see."

Terelle could see the sheer confusion on not only Dain's face, but on the expressions of the other two as well.

"He has magic boots that make it possible. Splat has had them since our second adventure together," she laughed a bit at that thought. "It was hilarious when he first found out their ability, especially as he learned how to use them."

"Yeah, me get many headaches before boots act right for me."

"And as far as keeping up goes, he has learned to slow way down to accommodate me and my pace. His normal stride would keep up with a horse's canter quite easily,"

Terelle explained.

"Me can run fast for long time," Splat announced proudly.

"Now, if we are all settled, we should get ready to go," Terelle announced.

The companions were already at the crossroads in town and it was late morning. With plenty of daylight, and everyone outfitted, it was just time to quit procrastinating.

"Dinly, would you like to lead the way?" Terelle asked as she mounted her steed.

Reluctantly, Dinly conceded and led the group on their way to Valley's Edge.

****

With the sky showing signs of precipitation soon, and the abundance of fall colored trees falling behind them, the thinly treed area started to show clumps of thick evergreen forest before them. The companions had been traveling for two days now and were seemingly climbing in elevation with each step.

In the distance, mountains came into view, some with snow covering the peaks like caps on the heads of Giants. Streams were everywhere in this area, as was wildlife such as deer, horses, and oxen. There were farms scattered throughout the region, some with cattle, some with sheep, and a few just growing food crops with maybe some chickens or ducks raised for meat. Rabbits were everywhere, almost in the same numbers as prairie dogs. It was evident that this was a place where one shouldn't have to worry about going hungry.

"Dinly?" Terelle asked, "With all of this out here, why did you have to eat fish?"

"I don't have the skills or equipment to catch any of them, and I had to have cold camps in case someone went by...I didn't want smoke from a fire to give me away."

"That makes sense, but things are changing for you. We will have to get you a few more items at the next store we come to and teach you how to live off the land."

"Can you teach me too?" an intrigued Trina asked.

"Yes, of course. It's a skill we should all have. How about you Dain?"

Dain looked uncomfortable and embarrassed as he hesitantly replied, "I might need a refresher course, if you don't mind."

Terelle could see that Dain was too proud to admit that he had no clue about how to harvest his own food.

"It's settled then. Splat and I will work with you all and teach you how to feed yourselves in the wilderness. It's easier than you think, but it does require patience and practice."

"How much will this extra gear weigh?" Dinly asked as she thought about the weight of her already bulky pack.

"Only a few ounces. Wire will add a couple of ounces more than string, but it will last much longer. You can choose which one you want."

Dinly was satisfied with that answer and was pleased that she had a say in the extra materials that she'd be carrying in her pack.

The very next morning, after only two hours or so of travel, they could see a man lying on the roadside. He wasn't moving, and even from a distance, the situation didn't appear to be right.

As they approached, Dinly called out, "I know that man. He drove the supply wagon I got the fish from."

They all stopped and Terelle, as she usually did, took charge.

"Nobody moves and keep your eyes peeled! I'm going to see if he is okay and try to figure out what happened."

She gingerly dismounted, trying not to further disturb the scene. She took in many things through her eyes, scanning the surrounding ground, as she carefully approached the man and then checked to see if he was still alive. He still had a pulse and was breathing.

"He'll live, but he's going to have one terrible headache. It looks as though several others waylaid him around half an hour ago. They took the wagon and headed to the right, up the ruts of that dirt farm road."

Trina asked, "How can you tell how long ago it was?"

"By looking at his injuries, how much bleeding and how much clotting. I want Splat and Dinly with me...we are going to get that wagon back. Dain, you and Trina get this man to the next town and get him some help."

"Are you sure it's a good idea to split up?" Dain questioned, worried that Terelle was walking into a situation where she'd be outnumbered.

"No, but if we don't that man may die, and I would really not like it if he did. Let's get moving," Terelle ordered.

Dain spent little time carefully laying the injured man across one of the pack horses and they proceeded to the next town. It was a short walk over a slight hill with the town in the next valley.

Terelle, Splat, and Dinly stuck to the trees as much as they could, always parallel with the tracks left by the wagon. They traveled over seven miles before Terelle noticed something else out of order. She halted Dinly and Splat with a hand signal and dismounted. Once Dinly had also dismounted, they tethered the two horses where they could eat some grass.

"What is it?" Dinly asked quietly.

"I smelled a whiff of smoke. They can't be far off. We will need to be as quiet as possible while approaching them. Splat, would you kindly fly slowly over the ground? You know your footsteps are heavy and easy to hear," she whispered.

"Okay," Splat said as quietly as he could. "Boots, fly!" he exclaimed in a hushed tone.

Dinly looked astonished as the boots brought the huge man off the ground without making a sound.

"Let's go," Terelle stated as she pulled her bow and knocked an arrow, leading them forward behind a screen of trees.

The camp consisted of an old log cabin with a couple of outbuildings. There was a woodshed, a small enclosed shed, likely for tools and such, a small corral with a lean-to for several horses, and an outhouse.

Without breaking cover, the three companions could see one guard keeping watch. They could also hear at least two voices in the cabin, and they saw that the wagon full of supplies was over near the lean-to.

The guard was a young blonde man who wore leather armor and carried a medium sized sword. Next to him was a bell he could ring if he needed to sound an alarm.

Not knowing how many bandits they were up against; they decided to wait and see if anything would give them more information to work with. If not for the heat of the day, Terelle could use her Infravision to examine the area. That wasn't an option and she hoped it wouldn't take until nightfall to find out how many they were up against.

While waiting, Dinly pulled some dehydrated apple slices from her pack, pulled the top off a water skin, and had a snack.

The companions were getting restless after an hour of waiting when the guard stood up, stretched and then walked toward the outhouse.

Seeing an opportunity, Terelle told the other two to stay put while she snuck up on the outhouse. She had to be careful as the bandit probably wouldn't be there very long.

When she got to the outhouse, she had to decide. The outhouse door was on the side that was visible from the cabin. If she entered, it may reveal her presence to those in the camp. However, to not enter the tiny building meant she would not get the information she needed.

She came around the side of the outhouse with the most cover. Having left her bow behind, she was now armed with a wicked looking dagger. Stealthily, she came around to the front and opened the door, quickly entering and confronting a surprised and defenseless wide-eyed man sitting with his pants down.

"Live or die?" she asked as the door closed behind her.

The shocked man started to react as her blade touched his neck.

"Live, live!" he said.

His sword was on the floor in its scabbard, attached to his lowered trousers by a stout belt. He could easily overpower this woman if she didn't have a knife to his throat, but she did have that advantage. Any wrong move on his part might inadvertently make her slice open his neck, and that just didn't figure to be a good plan.

"How many are in the cabin?"

"Five," he answered and swallowed hard.

"Are there any others around?"

"No, just the seven of us…."

The man instantly realized what he had done as she pushed the blade deep into his throat. He tried to lie to her.

She held his jaw up while he died, just in case he tried to yell with his last breath. Still not hearing any irregular noises from the cabin, she assumed she must not have been seen. Now she must move again.

Leaving the same way she came, Terelle hurried to cover. *Now is the tricky part...Where is the seventh man?* she thought as she worked her way back to her friends. Unsure of what to do at this point, she needed to think.

Terelle told her friends what she found out and asked for any input. Still whispering, Dinly told of her idea.

"I am a bit quieter than you...a lot smaller too. This will make it easier for me to go around the camp and find the other guard without him hearing me. The thing is, with one guard dead in the outhouse, I will need to hurry before somebody notices him being gone so long or someone else needs to use it."

"That's a good idea," Terelle said. "You go around and I'll sneak back up to the outhouse just in case someone else does show up. Splat, keep me covered."

They split up and put their plan into motion. Terelle made it back to the rear of the outhouse with no problem.

Dinly circled around the opening that the camp was in, never finding any trip wires or other traps or alarms. It wasn't until she had come nearly full circle that she could see the other guard. He was sitting in a lounge chair behind the cabin, directly under the one small window on that side. She could hear a faint snoring coming from the man. He was oblivious to her presence, and she just couldn't resist a chance to take out the man while he slept.

With ease, largely because of her diminutive stature, she avoided being seen from under the window and crept up on the man, blade already out and ready to conduct business. Quickly, she cuffed the man's mouth as her blade entered his neck. Pulling the blade out, Dinly watched as the dying man's blood pumped out of the sliver of a wound. He tried to bite her hand. Luckily for her, he no longer had the strength to do any real damage as the steady flow of blood decreased quickly and the light faded from his eyes.

Terelle didn't know whether she should ready her bow or keep her dagger out. It had been several minutes and Dinly had surely reached the other side by now, yet there was no sign of her. Thinking a bit more, she decided that that was a good thing, for if she could notice the Halfling, then someone else could too.

She was thinking this through when two men came out of the cabin. One started around the cabin while the other one seemingly started searching the yard. To Terelle, he appeared to focus his eyes on the outhouse.

Can he see me? Terelle thought, starting to bring on an unsure panic attack. *Breathe...calm down. He's just going to see if the other guard is in the outhouse. Shit!* She suddenly realized. *He's going to find the dead man in there!*

Normally very calm and reserved, she knew that this could put Dinly in a serious bind. She quickly reviewed her options and decided to just wait until the man made his way to the outhouse and then ambush him. Terelle would have to come from the opposite side this time, and her timing would have to be perfect. It was a workable plan, but then she heard the other man on the other side of the cabin call out.

Dinly's work here was done. She wiped her blade clean and snuck toward the trees when she heard another man call out.

"Hey Herb, are you sleeping again?" the man hollered when he turned the corner and noticed his buddy apparently snoozing in the lazy chair.

With his back almost completely toward her, Dinly quietly ran behind the new man. She was almost in striking distance when he saw the blood.

"Alert, al…" the man yelled, the second word cut short from a sword sunk deep into his back as he started to turn. To the man's credit, he pulled his sword halfway out of the scabbard before his arm quit working.

Dinly had barely sunk the blade between the man's vertebrae before he tried to turn. If he had turned a split second earlier, she would have missed the killing blow. Even so, his turning did throw her to the left where she hit the back of the log cabin, knocking the wind from her lungs. Dazed, she watched the man try to walk, stumble, and fall flat on his face. It made a dull sound, like a sack of potatoes dropped onto the floor.

"Hey Herb, are you sleeping again?" the farthest of the two men called out as he started to round the corner to the back of the cabin.

"Whew!" Terelle thought, "That was too close."

The man closest to her was only feet away from opening the door to the outhouse.

"Hey Bill, you in there?"

He reached for the door as Terelle rounded the back corner of the outhouse.

"Bill?" he called again and opened the door as Terelle unknowingly closed to within a couple of feet of the man.

Before Terelle could pounce, the man gasped as he, and Terelle, heard another man shout, "Alert, Al…" loudly.

The man closed the door with his left hand while drawing his sword with his right. As the door was closing, Terelle filled the space, dagger in hand as she swung it downward. The dagger was aimed to go behind the upper rib, but the man jumped back enough that she only creased the flesh of his chest.

"Help!" he called as he raised his sword.

Now Terelle was in real trouble. In a dagger versus a sword contest, the man definitely had the upper hand. She jumped backward at his first swing, the impact of it made a scraping sound. It was lucky that his sword only cut into her armor, just missing her flesh.

The man swung the sword again and she used all her strength and skill to try and block the blow. The impact knocked the dagger from her numbed hands, and she fell backward onto her back. She was now lying helplessly on the ground.

He knew he had her dead to rights, and she was at his mercy. The man looked over Terelle with lust that was fed by the fact that she was dressed provocatively, as she always was. She had on partial plate armor over leather, and her legs were uncovered from the thigh down to her shin guards. Her arms were likewise uncovered and her breastplate form fitting. The man stood over her, enthralled by her beauty and started thinking about the fun he could have with her as a slave. He started to smirk until he saw her smile back. He glanced over his right shoulder just in time to see a giant maul coming downward onto his head.

"Splat!" The noise of the maul doing its work was fairly disgusting. Blood, guts, tissue, and broken bones were sent in all directions, messing up the beauty of his best friend, but saving her, too.

Three more armed men came out of the cabin. Splat readied himself for a fight and Terelle reclaimed her feet and pulled her sword. They looked at each other briefly, both covered in gore, and then charged towards the three men.

The men had never seen such a sight, and it made them change their minds. At the last second, they tried to surrender. Too little, too late. They may as well have fought, for the bloodlust was already too far gone for the pair coming at them.

Terelle thrust her sword into one man's chest cavity while Splat smashed his maul into one of the others.

Realizing too late that the men were surrendering, two of those men lost their lives. The third man fell to the ground and curled up in a fetal position. Even with rage coursing through their bodies, the companions couldn't kill the last bandit. All three may have been spared, but they didn't decide to surrender until Splat and Terelle were within mere feet of them. It wasn't a huge loss; there were two less brigands in the world.

Splat kept watch over the prisoner while Terelle went to find Dinly. She turned the corner to the back of the cabin as Dinly was pulling her short sword from the second dead man's back.

"You look like crap!" Terelle called out.

Dinly glanced over at her new friend, smiling as she retorted, "Oh yeah? Try looking in a mirror. You don't look so hot yourself."

It took over two hours for the three companions to

clean up, gather anything useful, load the wagon, and hitch up the team of horses.

Terelle drove the wagon while Dinly rode her horse and led Terelle's horse. Splat watched over the prisoner who walked behind the wagon with his hands tied at the wrists. HE was not allowed to clean up. With the loss of his bladder control and soiling himself, nobody wanted to be too close to him, but they made him stay in his own stink.

It was nearly nightfall before the three companions and the prisoner made it to town. It was the very town that Dinly had run from only weeks ago.

At the sound of the wagon, Dain, Trina, and the Sheriff walked out into the street. The Sheriff recognized Dinly and immediately became angry and exerted his authority.

"You! I thought I told you to never come back here!"

"Sheriff," Dinly pleaded, "I've changed my ways and have come to pay any debts I may owe."

The Sheriff pointed to the building he and the others had come out of.

"There's a man you owe a bag of smoked fish to in there, and you owe me an outrageous amount for me feeding you all those times I put you in jail."

"How much?"

"What?"

"How much do I owe you?"

"It must be upwards of three gold, last I counted."

Dinly took out four gold and handed it to the Sheriff, saying, "Just in case you forgot anything."

"But...well...uh...how did you get this? You stole it, didn't you?"

"No, she didn't," Terelle told the Sheriff. "She has earned her money just like the rest of us. She even helped us retrieve this wagon from a band of brigands, the last of which is this man," she finished as she pointed to the prisoner.

"Adam!" the Sheriff called out loudly. "If you can walk, you may want to see this."

The man from the road carefully walked to the doorway, a large bandage wrapped around most of his head.

"My wagon?" the confused man exclaimed. "How can this be?"

Terelle answered, "We came upon your body on the road. I sent Dain and Trina," she pointed as she spoke, "ahead with you for medical treatment while the three of us retrieved the wagon and horses. We also got rid of the gang of bandits, of which this prisoner is the last of."

"And that is the girl who stole your fish," the Sheriff mentioned.

"I was starving at the time, but I will pay you for the

bag and the half loaf of bread," Dinly told the injured man.

"It cost me four silver for the bag of fish and a copper for the bread...but you and your friends saved me and brought back the horses, wagon, and all the supplies...You owe me nothing, little one."

"Not all of the supplies are here," Terelle told the man. "The brigands ate some of it before we got to them."

By this time, Dinly had walked to the man, put her hand into a bag, and then held her hand out.

"Here! I want you to know I paid my debt in full," she insisted as she handed him a gold round and two silvers.

"But this is, is…" the man stammered.

Terelle walked up and handed the man two gold rounds.

"I hope this will cover whatever that man and his cohorts used."

"I'm sure it will," the man beamed.

Dinly then walked back to the Sheriff and handed him a small sack of coins.

"This is to be given to each home in town. There are four silver for each home to cover any food I may have stolen from them."

The Sheriff had an astonished look on his face as he accepted the bag.

"You truly have changed! I don't know what to say."

"Just say you accept that I'm sorry for stealing food to stay alive and that I'm welcome in town again," Dinly said to the Sheriff with a smile on her small face.

"All that and more," the Sheriff replied.

"Good!" Terelle added. "Now that that's settled, we can go back home."

"Are you sure you must go? It's getting dark and I might ask if you could help me with another problem I have," the Sheriff told the companions.

"I'll tell you what Sheriff," Terelle answered, "We'll stay the night and get something warm to eat, and you can tell us about it in the morning."

"So, this whole trip here was to set things right?" the Sheriff asked Dinly.

"Yes. I never wanted to steal from innocent people, but I was starving after my family was run out of town and their inheritance was stolen. Now that I'm doing something with my life, I wanted to come back and clear my name, but it was also my companions who wanted me clear of any charges or negative past that may hound me."

"Well, your name is now clear here. Shall we talk about this other problem I have?"

Terelle answered his question with a question.

"So, what is this other problem anyway?"

The Sheriff turned very serious as he laid out his proposition. The companions perceived seriousness when the pitch and tone of his voice changed as he spoke.

"We've had Goblin attacks at three farms on the far side of the valley. At first it was just some missing livestock. That was annoying and worrisome, enough, but the attack two nights ago included the loss of old man Harold. He was an old friend of mine."

"What are the logistics if we take the job?" Terelle

inquired with interest in her voice.

"Free room and board are all I can offer, plus the few gold rounds you just gave me," the Sheriff apologetically explained.

"What about anything we find?"

"If you run across Harold's wedding band, his widow would like it back...but anything else is yours."

The Sheriff looked pleadingly at each of the companions.

Terelle then asked the question out loud that was on everybody's mind.

"Does anyone NOT want to take on this job?"

There was no reply from the companions, which was the consent she needed to move forward with the Sheriff.

"Okay, I think you have us for the job. When do we start?"

"It's not long after breakfast," the Sheriff stated the obvious. "How about now?"

"Can you take us to Harold's farm and let us look around?"

"Yes, I can be ready in fifteen minutes or so."

The farm was typical of the other farms in the region. It was relatively small, consisting of a house, barn, and outbuildings. And there was livestock and crops in a field.

"This is where his body was discovered and four sheep were found missing," the Sheriff told the companions.

"They're old, but the tracks lead toward those mountains," Terelle pointed, showing the Sheriff where she suspected the attacks came from. "Goblins aren't known for their stealth."

About this time, a lady in her sixties came from the house and walked toward them. Though it took her a couple of minutes to arrive, it would have been rude to leave as she approached, so the companions stayed and politely waited.

"Hello Sheriff," the widow started. "Who are your friends? I don't remember seeing them around, except the little one there. I remember feeding you a few times, I do."

"Yes ma'am," Dinly did her best to curtsy with all her gear on. "And now I'm trying to pay people around here back for any wrong doings I may have done."

The Sheriff then pulled out the purse of silver and took out four silver rounds and handed them to the lady.

"She sure did! Gave me this for everyone, paid me back for all her trouble, and she and her friends saved Jones and his delivery, too."

"My goodness, things must be looking up for you. But tell me, why are you and your friends here now? Surely the Sheriff could handle giving me a few coins."

The Sheriff looked a bit cautious as he told her, "I've

hired them to track down the Goblins, and hopefully, get rid of them."

"Oh my! I do hope you're careful," the widow said and then looked directly at Splat. "But with a big brute like him with you, I'm sure you will be alright."

The Sheriff gave the widow more information.

"I told them I'm paying for room and board, so you might see them come and go several times."

"Nonsense!" the widow protested. "They can stay here, though I'll let you help with food. I can put you all in our spare room…ah, except for you big boy…you won't fit. You'll have to sleep in the barn I'm afraid."

"That's okay," Terelle tried to comfortably inform the widow. "We sleep where he sleeps. Splat and I are used to using barns. It's a common situation for us."

"I meant no offense," the widow said apologetically.

"None taken…none at all. We thank you for your generous offer. It will save us a couple of hours round trip. The barn will be just fine Mrs…?"

"Tucker…Emily Tucker."

After introductions were completed, the companions, minus Splat, mounted their horses and they all headed in the direction Terelle had pointed out. The Sheriff stuck around for a bit before leaving his friend's widow to take care of her farm.

The companions came to the fence and noticed a temporary fix that would keep sheep in but wouldn't stop much else.

"Looks like we can just disconnect things quickly here, go through and then put things back together again. After this, we will go around," Terelle instructed.

Once through, and with the fence once again put back together, the companions set off toward the hills with Terelle leading the way. They watched for any signs of the Goblins having gone in this direction.

"If their trail stays this easy to follow, it should lead us right to them," Terelle announced.

Focused on the task at hand, and wary of the potential danger ahead, there wasn't much talking between the companions for a while.

Dinly was wondering what it would be like to fight Goblins. She had never seen one before and wasn't sure what she would be up against. She hoped she was up to the task.

Trina had heard of Goblins before, briefly, but all she had heard was that they were slick-skinned creatures of nightmares that would eat a person alive if they caught you.

Dain was looking forward to his first real test against the slimy little green skins. He had heard of them in stories of combat and pride, and he had been told of Dwarves killing hundreds of goblins in a single day. Dain wasn't sure if the numbers were exaggerated from too much ale, but he planned to find out for himself just how tough, or not, that these Goblins were.

Splat was wondering how his new friends would act when up against these Goblins they were after. For him, it was no problem; he had killed plenty of Goblins in his lifetime. Only the rare Goblin Cleric made his stomach churn. He really hated the Goblin Clerics.

Terelle concentrated on watching for sign so they would stay on track and find these miserable little creatures. The sadness in the eyes of the widow and the Sheriff were enough to make her want to kill every Goblin out there. With the prisoner now in the Sheriff's jail, and a local place to sleep, things had started to look up for her and her friends.

As the companions made their way closer to the hills, the once sparse tree coverage started to become much denser. It was getting to the point where the group had to start going around trees, instead of traveling the nice straight line the Goblins had been leaving. The trees now became mixed, with evergreens slowly dominating the area and becoming a much taller forest than it was only a few miles back. Despite the impending job, the group relished the fresh mountain air and the intense smell of the trees and earth. Mindful of potential danger, the companions continued to climb in elevation.

By mid-morning the companions were in the rolling hills of the forest when Terelle slowed her horse, looked around, and then stopped.

"There is a problem with the trail," she told the others.

"What happened to it?" Dain asked.

"It has run into a mass of foot and hoof traffic that goes in all directions. There are so many prints that I can't distinguish between them all. They must have a camp around here somewhere. We need to find it, but first, we need to find some cover and tether the horses."

Dinly turned at a very slight noise coming from behind and to the left of the companions. She noticed a slight movement amongst some of the boulders that looked like they grew right out of the hillside.

Keeping her eyes trained in that direction, she murmured, "Hey guys...I think we have a visitor at our left rear location."

The companions turned, and Terelle spoke softly, "That is our seven o'clock position...and it looks like one very scared Goblin. Nobody make any sudden moves...I've got this."

With her body mostly shielded, just by chance, from

the Goblin's sight by Splat, she grabbed her bow and nocked the first of two arrows she had brought to the forefront. She drew back as she nudged her horse forward a couple of feet, aimed, and launched the arrow all in a split second.

The Goblin rose to run just in time to receive an arrow through its chest. The creature dropped like a stone.

"I guess we should go see what we just got ourselves into," Terelle stated in a matter of fact manner as she dismounted from her horse.

She had already nocked the other arrow and was looking around for another target. Seeing none, she carefully moved toward the dead or dying Goblin.

It was dead. Terelle retrieved her arrow and quickly searched the body. Besides a dagger and a few minor coins from another realm, there was nothing of value to take.

"That was a heck of a good shot," Dain stated.

"No, it wasn't. Unfortunately, I was aiming for his head," Terelle retorted, "I wasn't expecting him to stand quite so fast."

Trina pointed out a cave entrance that was behind them as one would look toward the Goblin. From any other view, it was unnoticeable because of the way the boulders were arranged. Even looking in the correct direction, you had to look closely to notice it.

Splat grunted.

"What's wrong with him?" Dinly asked.

Terelle gave a knowing look and explained, "He doesn't like caves. They are sometimes too small for him to fit through."

"Oh...I guess that makes sense."

Terelle approached the cave entrance, adjusting her vision as she stepped carefully through the opening and into the dimness beyond. She brought her head back out.

"There's a passage here, and it's lit with torches every so often. We should drag the dead Goblin from here, find a place for the horses, and then see where this leads. We may find what we are looking for in here."

Splat grabbed the dead creature, and the companions left the way they came. They went a good quarter mile before leaving the trail and finding a place to picket the horses where they would have plenty to eat, a creek to drink from, and still be out of sight from the trail the Goblins had used. It was then time to go back.

****

"It's your turn!"

"I just had a turn yesterday! Why do I have to have another turn already?"

"Because Dribin say so and it's time for Tordo to go back to guttin' the mutton."

"I could do that!"

"Yeah, but you ruin too much. Now go take Tordo's place like you were told."

"Go relieve Tordo! Go relieve Tordo! I'll relieve Tordo all right, damned muttonhead Josko, I hope you chokes on your mutton," the lonely Goblin mumbled his complaints on the way to his guard post. "Maybe I'll tell Tordo he's been kicked out of the tribe and he'll just leave. Ah, that would be so nice."

The Goblin climbed a long passageway, noticing that several torches needed replacing soon, before exiting the cavern to look for Tordo.

It figures he's not around when he's supposed to be, he thought. Now where did he go off to?"

****

The companions crept around the corner, not sure what to expect as it had been nearly an hour since they had found the Goblin and the cave entrance. Everybody was ready for a conflict in case an alarm had been sounded.

Terelle spotted another Goblin that appeared to be by

itself. She raised her hand for the others to stop, nocked an arrow, and let it fly toward the creature. The arrow went right through its spinal column from back to front as the Goblin was turned away from the party. It let out a slight yelp before falling over in the same general area as the first Goblin died in, and it looked as if this one had just spied the blood that had been left behind by his dead comrade.

Once the companions had checked for more Goblins and found none, Terelle again went over and retrieved her arrow and collected some coins and another dagger.

Nobody had a problem with Terelle collecting the majority of the coins for the group. This had been agreed upon earlier in the week, and the newbies knew some of their money and possessions had come from Terelle's own finances.

Terelle once again checked inside the cave entrance and found no noticeable danger, before waving in her companions.

The actual entrance was a bit of a squeeze for Splat, the small protrusions of rock doing their best to scratch the surface layer of his skin in places.

"Ugh, tight fit. Hope whole place not like this."

Splat turned sideways to enter the cavern.

"No big buddy," Terelle informed him, "it opens up nice once you get through the entrance."

"Maybe move boulder now, easier to leave?" Splat suggested.

"No, others might notice and attack from behind," Terelle explained quickly.

"Humph!"

The companions started down the damp algae-strewn hallway, noticing many of the torches burning low. As they passed the fourth sputtering torch, Dain pulled a new one from his pack, lit it from the old one, and placed the new one into the sconce attached to the tunnel wall.

"What are you doing?" Terelle asked in a whisper.

"We all need to see. They have these too close together, but every other one needs replacing or we will end up in the dark," Dain answered.

"Then we use the ones already in the alcoves, instead of our own."

She showed him how to find the small areas near each sconce with half a dozen cheaply made torches in each of them.

"Good idea! Why didn't you show me those earlier?" Dain tried to keep his voice low.

"I wasn't thinking about changing the torches," Terelle answered.

"I can run back and change the ones back there that need it if you want me to," Dinly said.

"No, we need to stick together down here," Terelle advised the Halfling. "Did you notice we are headed downward now?"

Nobody perceived the change in elevation except for Dain who was raised under the rock of mountains.

It was decided that Dain would replace every other torch from the first he had done, and Dinly would replace the alternate in front of him, so no one person would be slowed down too much. The sconces were approximately fifty feet apart, and though it slowed the group down a bit, it might help their escape if they needed one. It also aided with them being able to see if any enemies were coming from behind them, instead of the torches dying and leaving them in a wake of darkness.

Dinly and Dain got into a rhythm as they changed out the dying or dead torches, leapfrogging each other as they progressed down the tunnel. After they changed out seven of the torches, Terelle suddenly nocked an arrow and fired in one swift motion. Nobody had even seen the Goblin down the hall, except for Terelle herself.

"What was that?" Trina asked.

"A Goblin had just changed a torch down there and I figured he would come this way, so he had to be silenced," she quietly explained as she pulled another arrow. "Let's go see what we have down there."

The companions picked up their pace but continued to change out the old torches in the two-hundred-foot distance between them and the dead Goblin.

When they arrived, it was what was sort of expected by now. There was a dead body, a dagger, and a few cheap coins from a nearby Kingdom. Terelle retrieved her arrow.

"Nice of him to have changed the torches to this point for us, wouldn't you say?" Terelle commented with a sly grin on her face.

"Less work for us!" Dinly answered.

"Sure beats changing them ourselves," Terelle added. "Let's go!"

They didn't have to go far. Another few hundred feet and they could see an opening off to their right. It was easy to tell that the room was occupied with all the noise coming from it.

Terelle quick-looked into the room and found seven Goblins that she could see in a room with close to a dozen piles of debris that was probably bedding for these creatures. She held up seven fingers while holding her bow with three. She waved Splat and Dain in front of her. Dain went to her left and Splat to her right, and Terelle motioned for Dinly to watch their backs. Trina would follow Terelle into the room.

Once ready, Dain and Splat charged into the room and

immediately found a cluster of surprised combatants. Terelle swooped in behind Dain and started firing arrows at the furthest targets, while Trina came in behind Splat and cast a spell to kill the only enemy in the middle area between Splat and Dain.

Dain started to swing his axe at the first of two Goblins in front of him, slicing the creature in half from head to groin. The other Goblin had just pulled his weapon when Dain swung again, taking off the nimble arm that held the crude dagger. By his third swing, Dain had dispatched his targets.

Splat had two Goblins in front of him as well. His immense size was a study in contrasts when compared to the small and relatively weak creatures who were a true threat when operating as a pack. He went on the offensive but missed with his first swing. The shock in the eyes of those two Goblins quickly turned to grim smiles of sorts from the miss. Both pulled weapons and tried to jump at Splat when his backswing caught the first of them, knocking the instantly dead and crushed bag-o-bones Goblin into the other, knocking him off balance. The next swing was overhead at a dazed foe that couldn't move out of the way. The only thing left after the maul finished its downward plunge was a grisly smear of blood, guts, and bone fragments on the floor of the cave.

Terelle fired three quickly aimed arrows into the two targets she had her sights on, the first shot flying true. The second arrow struck an arm of her second Goblin, and her third shot finished the job. As the companions were finished with the battle, another Goblin called out loudly as he rose from a pile on the floor and tried to attack Dain.

Though the attack was a surprise, Dain easily sidestepped the attempt and used his axe to cut an arm and shoulder from the attacker. He stepped over to the mortally wounded creature and finished him off.

With the battle finally over, Terelle went to the back of the room to retrieve her arrows and found that the first creature she hit had landed at an angle, snapping the shaft on that arrow. She retrieved the two parts, then the two arrows from the other dead Goblin before checking the bodies.

Dinly came in as Terelle finished searching the other bodies she had dispatched.

"More coming from further in!" Dinly warned.

The companions quickly organized in a reverse of their entry except that Dinly now stood between Terelle and Trina, just forward of them, ready to defend against any enemies that broke through Splat and Dain.

They no more than took their positions than Goblins started coming into the room. Like the beginning of flood waters, several of them came through the entrance at once.

Dain cut through one and into another with his first swing, while Splat used the same side swing in reverse with the slightly pointed side of his maul. This crushed the first Goblin and pushed two more backward.

With the mass of creatures rushing into the room, two Goblins made it through only to be blasted by a spell from Trina and two arrows from Terelle, one in the shoulder and the second through the head.

The second wave pressed the attack with similar results, but there were a couple of differences. Only one Goblin came in where Splat was and three broke through the middle.

Terelle dispatched one quickly and a second only feet from her. The third one ran toward Trina, who hadn't yet prepared a new spell. Seeing her new friend in danger, Dinly jumped in front of the mage to defend her, figuring correctly that Terelle could more easily handle her situation, what with all her experience. Dinly parried with the Goblin for two swings before seeing an opening. She slid her short sword through her opponent's defense and stabbed him in the upper right chest. She pushed with all her strength.

Her sword became stuck and the Goblin tried one last attack before death came to it. As the Goblin's dagger was coming toward her, the beast lost his footing and fell, his legs cut off above the knees. Dinly had barely seen the flash of the axe blade flying into and out of her vision.

Dain had saved her as she had likely saved Trina.

"One of dem got away," Splat announced.

"He'll be going for reinforcements," Terelle breathily acknowledged. "Dinly, stand watch again. Everyone else gather weapons and search the bodies."

She laid the coin bag on the ground near the center of the room for all to add coin to. Terelle retrieved her arrows first, and then started searching the bodies.

With four of the companions working at it together, they easily gathered everything worth taking in a short amount of time. Amongst the twenty-six weapons were four short swords and twenty-two daggers. The short swords must have been from section leaders of sorts, and those four also had a little more of the coins they kept finding amongst these Goblins. Since there wasn't any word yet from Dinly, the other companions started searching the room for anything of value.

Amongst all the debris, Terelle found a piece of wood that she was ninety percent sure was a wand of some sort, and she tucked it away for future investigation. Besides that, nothing else of interest or value was in the room. There was a table and five chairs of poor workmanship in the room that were the real highlights compared to the rest of the garbage in the chamber.

Once they had finished, upon Terelle's insistence, they all took a drink of water and caught their collective breath. It took several minutes before Dinly popped back into the room with the news that another pack of Goblins were on the way.

"Okay guys," Terelle ordered as she started moving into her position, "let's get ready for another go around with these foul beasts!"

They waited twice as long as they figured it would take before anything happened. When it did, it was as before, but with one additional factor. As the Goblins stormed through the tunnel entrance, so did six poorly aimed crossbow bolts. Luckily, none of the bolts found their targets as the companions fought and defeated a wave of seven goblins before another eight charged in a rapid second wave.

Six more crossbow bolts flew through the air, one finding a home in Trina's left arm this time. Trina called out in pain and her arm hung limp.

Terelle had to drop her bow and draw her sword as Dinly was trying to hold two Goblins at bay. It looked like she might not win the exchange. The Goblins were now just too close for her to get any kind of shot off, so Terelle had to resort to melee combat.

A third wave of shrieking creatures kept Splat and Dain

busy while yet another round of bolts flew into the room. Two bolts hit targets, the first landing in the back of a Goblin fighting with Dinly, giving her a reprieve. The other bolt hit Terelle in the breastplate and bounced off, leaving a slight dent in the armor. It was lucky for her that these weren't the best crossbows or bolts and that the Goblins using them weren't very good with them.

Terelle dispatched one of the Goblins trying to kill Dinly, while Dinly finished off another that had inadvertently been shot by his own clan.

Dain and Splat had done an incredible job of stopping the third and fourth waves of attackers before the remaining Goblins started to retreat. It was feverish combat that was both exhilarating and exhausting. They hoped for a reprieve.

Picking up her bow as she scabbarded her sword, Terelle ran to the entrance of the room. Nocking an arrow, she quick-looked down the tunnel. She entered the passage and started sending arrows down range.

"Dain, come with me, quickly," Terelle demanded.

The two of them ran down the tunnel toward several Goblin bodies that littered the ground.

"I can't believe it! You killed five of them and wounded two! How many arrows did you fire?" Dain asked.

"Nine!" She looked disgusted. "I can't believe I missed twice," she grumbled. "Grab the bodies and weapons, and then drag them back to the others. I'll make sure they don't have as many crossbows to play with."

It took the two of them a few minutes to bring the bodies and weapons into the room, but they got the job done.

****

I don't believe it! I've never seen Goblins fight with numerous crossbows and use strategy while doing so! Terelle had been thinking as they gathered what was useful.

"Splat, I'll need you to carry this heavy bag of blades and crossbows."

They had gained seventeen short swords, fifty-five daggers, and six crossbows with twenty bolts each after gathering those that had been fired.

Trina wasn't doing really well, but her arm had been cleaned and bandaged. The wound from the bolt wasn't life threatening as long as it didn't get infected, so they took just enough time to gather what they had looted and planned their escape. If the wound had been more severe, they would have just left without gathering things, or they would have used some form of magic to keep her alive. But the wound being what it was, allowed for them to plan an exit that would net them quite a few weapons and a pile of coin.

It was a workable plan, as long as another group of Goblins didn't show up before they could leave.

"I think we put a dent in their numbers," Terelle told the others. "They might not want to attack us for a while, so they can organize a better attack next time. Let's take this chance to get ourselves out of here and regroup."

Terelle was seriously mad that she not only missed a few shots but lost a couple of her arrows too. It also irked her that Trina was injured. No amount of loot was worth the potential loss of a party member if it could be avoided.

Dain had asked about her getting upset about losing arrows and Terelle notified him that her arrows were made by an expert and they cost twice as much as normal arrows. They were also much more accurate than any other arrows you could buy in normal shops. Replacing a lost or damaged arrow was possible, but not favorable.

The coin bag was heavy now, and even though the coins were mostly zinc, copper, and silver, it was still a good day's pay.

"Let's get out of here!" Terelle told the others as she picked up the coin bag and placed it in her pack.

"Hold on a minute," Dain spoke. "Do you have another large sack?"

"Yes, why?" Terelle asked.

"I have an idea. It won't make us rich, but it'll irritate

the rest of the Goblins a little more," Dain said with a wink and a smile.

Terelle pulled another large sack out of her backpack and handed it to him, wondering what he had on his mind.

"Okay...here you go."

Dain took the rear-guard position and asked that the group not leave as rapidly as they could have. Terelle led the way out of the system of tunnels as Dain stopped at each alcove near the torch sconces and grabbed every unlit torch as they retreated.

7

All the companions sat around a table in the barn, except for Trina who was laying down resting. Terelle was using a ball peen hammer that was in a tool chest to try to smooth out her breastplate. Unfortunately, she wasn't having any luck and was getting frustrated.

"You should be glad you had good, hard steel or that plate wouldn't have stopped the bolt from going into you," Dain stated.

"I don't like the divot," she punctuated the statement as she pounded the breastplate. "It's rubbing against my chest and I now have a bruise there from being shot."

Mrs. Tucker had helped prepare a big dinner after they had arrived back. She also helped Terelle do a better job on Trina's arm. Having access to boiling water and a few herbs made it possible for Terelle to make a poultice, instead of either waiting a couple of weeks or using magic to heal the wound. The poultice would promote healing, and Trina's arm would be back to normal in three to four days. This would allow for plenty of time to rest up.

"How many Goblins do you think are left?" Dinly asked Terelle.

"I'm not sure...I've heard of clans that surpass 500 of the creatures, and that's just the combatants, mind you, not the women and children. We took out eighty to ninety of them today, but I doubt they are done with."

You mean there could be more than five times the number we fought today?"

"That's what I'm saying."

"Today was hard work. I don't think I've been so scared in all of my life."

"Oh? Goblins are easy compared to some of the things Splat and I have been up against."

"There's no way I'm ready for anything harder," Dinly shook her head.

"Not yet, maybe, but you'll get more training, treasure, and exposure to what we do and then you'll feel more confident."

"I sure hope so!" Dinly replied with a hint of doubt.

****

The companions stayed at Mrs. Tucker's house for four days. Even though Trina's arm was looking fine after only three days, they wanted one more, just to be sure. Trina mentioned that her arm still felt "strange," but she had full mobility and no obvious signs of a wound, just a small scar.

Terelle had pulled out the bag of coins on the third day, and everyone helped sort and count what they had come out with. Most of the coins had come from a neighboring Kingdom, but not all. Luckily the exchange rate was fairly equal between that Kingdom and the one they lived in. They brought back 423 zinc rounds and ovals, 341 copper rounds and ovals, 217 silver rounds and ovals, 19 composite rounds and ovals, and 3 gold ovals. It was a lot of coins, but the total value wasn't very impressive. Still, it was something of a start. When combined with the weapons they collected, it was a worthwhile day and they did rid the world of quite a few Goblins. But their job was not finished. Now, it was time to go back and do some more good.

The companions left their horses in the same location as they did the first time and started toward the cave entrance.

About halfway there, Terelle stopped them with a hand signal to do so.

Something isn't right, she thought to herself and started looking around. *There...napping behind a tree...and there conked out behind a boulder...and up there, snoring in the branches* she mentally mapped out the locations of the Goblins. She prided herself in locating the creatures.

It was a good thing Goblins were inherently lazy and

get bored easily. The problem wasn't the three she had seen, it was, however, the potential for the many she still didn't know about. She waved Trina up to her.

"Can you cast a spell to see how many of our enemies are around us?" she whispered.

"No, I'm sorry, that is above my skill level at this time," Trina whispered in reply.

Trina didn't even see the three that Terelle saw.

Terelle was a little disappointed, but they had to do something, so she formulated a plan.

"Okay, you and Dinly get behind trees for cover. Tell Splat and Dain to expect an ambush. I'm going to try to take out those that I can first."

Terelle gave Trina and Dinly a moment to quietly find cover and for Dain and Splat to prepare for battle before pulling out four arrows. She nocked the first arrow and tried to figure where a fourth Goblin might be when looking at the position of the other three. She thought to herself, *There should be one right about …there!* Again, she impressed herself with finding a fourth Goblin, laying on a rock in a fetal position.

She chose to work from right to left, taking out the Goblin in the tree last. She would normally work in the opposite direction, taking out the Goblin with the height advantage first, but if the Goblin in the tree fell, the noise would likely wake the others and propel them into combat. She had faith that her friends could win the battle easily, but there would be a much better chance of an alarm being called out that way.

The first two shots flew perfectly, killing their targets instantly. As she fired the third arrow, however, her target rolled to one side. Though the arrow inflicted killing damage, it wasn't instantaneous, and the Goblin yelled in pain. Terelle took her fourth shot, now needing more than ever to take out the Goblin in the tree. That Goblin started to shake the cobwebs of sleep away when it was pierced through the heart and tumbled to the ground.

Thwack! There was a near miss above Dinly's head.

Of course! Terelle thought when she heard the crossbow bolt imbed itself into the rough bark of the tree Dinly had hidden behind. *Of course, they would try to surround the companions with the trap. How many more were out there?* she wondered.

There were several animalistic yells from all around them, working to both terrify and inform the companions of the enemy's location.

"Come on, follow me!" Terelle called out. "Most of them are behind us and to the sides. We move forward!"

Crossbow bolts chased them as they advanced, and the lone Goblin in front of them fled for his life. He wasn't quite fast enough, as Terelle dropped him with an arrow.

They ran past the body on the way to find concealment.

After running the hundred-yard dash to a place where they could fight back from behind a large, downed tree, they stopped and turned around.

Splat turned to Dain and calmly asked, "Can you pull these out of me?"

Dain looked at his fairly new friend in awe before pulling three bolts out of the Giant's well-muscled back as gently, but as quickly, as possible.

"Ah! Thank you...them things hurt some," Splat commented.

The Goblins came at a rush. There must have been thirty of them in the first wave. Terelle dropped seven of them before having to change to her sword. She and Splat went into the middle of the melee and stood back to back, piling dead bodies all around them.

Trina cast a spell that killed two attackers in a beautiful ball of fire, then drew her two daggers and helped Dinly protect Dain's back as he killed several Goblins.

The battle was looking like a massacre when another thirty or so Goblins attacked. Preceding this wave, crossbow bolts again filled the air around the companions before the second group of attackers arrived.

As the companions fought on, all of them were getting tired, except for Splat, and all of them were sustaining wounds—minor cuts and a few crossbow bolts—that were painful, but didn't do enough damage to stop them from fighting.

Fatigued to the point of exhaustion, Dinly nearly dropped her short sword, and Trina was once again injured as she swung a dagger to fend off another Goblin with a short sword.

Dain couldn't help because he still had four creatures in front of him that were doing their best to wear him down with the nicks and stab wounds they inflicted.

Preoccupied with the hoard in front of them, they hadn't even noticed that a third wave had entered into combat. It was on the verge of overwhelming, and there was no time to get a break.

Trina got a lucky strike into the Goblin facing her, and she had a short moment to breathe. With her last burst of energy, she cast a spell on her two nearby companions and then dropped to the ground.

Dain and Dinly felt a pulse of energy flood through them, inspiring them to fight harder. Dinly immediately took out her combatant, and Dain pounded two in a matter of seconds. Dinly came around Dain's weaker side, and the two of them dispatched their immediate foes.

Splat and Terelle had moved a couple of times because of the piles of dead bodies around them. The companions hadn't even noticed, yet, that another twenty Goblins had joined the attack. They just kept fighting and hoped that it would end soon.

Several of this last bunch had crossbows slung across their backs, but they were now using blades in their attack. Terelle was wounded and tired when she noticed Dain heading her way, dropping a couple of Goblins along the way.

Small groups of attackers kept spilling into the war zone, but the numbers were diminishing, and the flow of creatures was slowing down.

Terelle fell to the ground.

8

Dain rushed to defend Terelle from two would-be attackers. As he took out those two, Splat bludgeoned the last three Goblins from in front of him.

"We need to get her to the others...she's hurt!" Dain called out.

Splat turned to see his friend on the ground. A dark light burned in Splat's eyes, and Dain took an involuntary step back from the look of pure rage that showed on the Giant.

"You take, I'll be there soon!"

There were a little more than a dozen Goblins left in sight, but it didn't matter to Splat. They could have numbered in the hundreds and he would have still taken his bloodlust-driven violence out on them. Splat stormed off to the closest Goblin as Dain picked up Terelle to carry her back behind the tree.

A loud roar emanated from Splat as he smashed the first of the remaining Goblins. As nicked and spackled with crossbow bolts as he was, Splat was a sight to behold.

Dain made it to the downed tree and set Terelle down softly on a patch of green grass.

"Watch her too and see what you can do for them, I'm going to go…." Dain stated but never finished because he fell to the ground.

Dinly also dropped to the ground. Trina's spell that had kept them going had finally worn off.

The lone Goblin couldn't believe his luck. First, he thought he was dead, and then he was sure the invading party would overrun him, or at least find him where he had landed when he tripped over a tree root. But here he was with four of them at his mercy, and the only one able to fight was off in the distance killing his family.

He snuck over to them, started to pull his dagger, and stood in the middle of the unconscious and helpless group. All of them would die by his hand. He would be the hero of his clan and get the best females as mates. Big dreams for such a weak creature. Dreams that wouldn't come to fruition.

A dagger entered his upper back, severing his line to life.

It was all Trina could do to put that dagger into the vile creature, and she had to wait until he stepped past her to get a good opportunity to eke out her one stabbing plunge. She had no more strength in her, and she hoped the effort she was able to muster was enough.

When Splat could find no more Goblins, he flew back to his companions, thankful for those magical boots he had. What he saw nearly killed him inside. All four of his companions looked dead to him. He had one magic potion that would partially heal someone, and he pulled it out of his haversack. In a delicate motion he took the stopper from the bottle and gently poured it down Terelle's mouth, a little every few seconds just like she had shown him, until the bottle was empty. Still he saw nothing happen.

Devastated, Splat started to cry. Terelle meant everything to him.

Was the dream worth all of this? He asked himself silently.

Terelle opened her eyes, slowly at first, looked to Splat and weakly said, "Hi handsome...thank you for saving me once again."

She then saw his tears and looked at the others.

"Are they...?"

"Don't know...don't know how to tell," he sobbed.

"Okay, big guy...I'll check them."

Terelle struggled to get up at first, but she was able to gain her footing with a great deal of effort. She was, however, a bit unsteady. She shuffled over and checked the other companions.

"They'll make it," Terelle comforted Splat, "but I'll have to use a potion on Trina."

She then dug into her backpack, found a healing potion, and then poured the liquid down Trina's throat.

Terelle sat and watched many of the smaller wounds heal and the larger wounds close, but not quite heal fully.

"She must have been closer to death than I thought," Terelle commented. "She will require time off, as will the rest of us. Right now, the three of them need rest. Actually, I still need rest too. Do you think if I pull the bolts out of you that you can stay on watch while we get some rest?"

"Yeah, me can for about three hours before I need rest...me hope nothing happens.

After a couple of hours, the companions started to stir. They stretched tight muscles and noticed several aches and pains. Terelle awoke because of the noise.

"What the heck happened?" Trina asked.

"It's called battle fatigue and we all have it," Terelle explained. "Splat has been watching out for all of us, however, he can go no longer...he needs to rest now while we watch for trouble."

She took a drink of water and had the others do so as well, including Splat.

"Dain, I want you to stay here with Splat while the three of us start rounding up anything of value and see just how many Goblins ambushed us."

"Sounds like a good plan!" Dain replied.

The three women spent over two hours piling up weapons, retrieving arrows and crossbow bolts, while also looking for any money the goblins may have had on hand. When the final count was done, there was between 130 and 140 dead Goblins, although all three women were somewhat unsure of the final amount due to the many unrecognizable body parts at some locations.

With several sacks of blades and another with eight crossbows and almost 20 bolts each, they decided they had accomplished their goals for the moment.

Terelle had two sacks of coins this time and held them up.

"We should all go back with our treasures and heal up once Splat is finished with his nap.

Dain couldn't hold it in anymore. He had been watching for Goblins but would occasionally look at Splat. He saw that Splat was healing quicker than any other creature he'd ever seen. It was like Splat possessed some sort of magical healing powers.

"How is it that he heals while he sleeps?"

"We all heal best when we sleep," Terelle hoped the questions would stop there.

"Yes, but we don't go from open wounds to wounds healed in an hour, not without magic of some sort."

"You have noticed that he isn't full-blooded Human, haven't you?"

"Yes, of course."

"He has Giant blood, as well, and has natural healing abilities because of it."

"I've also noticed that his maul is way too heavy for even me to do more than drag, and I'm exceedingly strong, even amongst my people," Dain looked curious.

"He was given that maul by his father, a Giant who can summon storms and lightning bolts, along with many other things. Splat can do all sorts of things that none of us can do, but he only does so when necessary because he wants to fit in with humans as much as possible. How would you like to be called a freak of nature?" Terelle looked at each of the other companions.

Dain thought for a second before giving his answer.

"I guess I wouldn't like it at all. I'd like to think I fit in somewhere."

"Well, there you go. Splat has feelings just like anyone else, and those feelings can be hurt as easily as anyone else's."

"I'm so used to seeing him so happy all the time. I just never connected the dots," Dain confessed. "I do kind of wish we could all heal like that, even if it meant being called a freak."

"So do I... more so than you know," Terelle commented as she placed the bags of coins into her backpack. "Now let's get ready to go. He'll be awake soon."

Twenty minutes later Splat awoke and looked around, remembering where he was.

"You okay big guy?" Dain asked.

"Uh huh, me okay."

"Good!" Terelle added. "I have some large sacks of weapons for you to carry to the horses."

"No problem," Splat cheerfully said as he looked at all the dead Goblins and smiled. "Looks like we win battle!"

"Yes buddy, we won this one, but we all need to get back and heal up. We got busted up pretty bad this round," Terelle informed him.

"Okay!" Splat said.

The companions gathered their things and started to leave, each person bearing part of the burden.

****

The companions made it back to Mrs. Tucker's farm without further incident. They were on edge and weary as they quietly trudged along. There wasn't much talking until they arrived at the barn and everyone started to relax.

Trina was the first to start a conversation by asking,

"Terelle?"

"Yes?"

"Are we always going to fight such horrific battles?" inquired Trina fearfully.

"What, these? These are easy battles. Granted these Goblins are a bit better armed and are using tactics unusual for their kind, but Goblins are easy to fight and kill. We are lucky you are getting your feet wet with them instead of some truly hard to fight enemies."

"You call these easy! I've been injured both times we went to fight them," Trina lashed out.

She couldn't believe that Terelle was calling these creatures EASY. They seemed to be anything but easy. Maybe one on one they were easy but fighting hordes of the creatures was a monumental task.

"Look at the number of them we have killed," Terelle tried to reason. "There are only five of us and we've killed well over 200 of them in two days of combat. There are many creatures and other enemies that would kill us all without even breaking a sweat."

"But…" Trina started and then was interrupted.

"But nothing! The three of you are very new to this line of work and what we are doing now will give you some much needed experience, but it is just the beginning. Splat and I have been doing this together for years and we still are nowhere close to calling ourselves experts."

"How long does it take?" a surprised Dinly asked.

Trina listened intently as she unbelted the sword she'd been wearing. It dangled from her right hand as she looked around for a place to stow it. Frustrated with the discussion, she tossed it onto a nearby table and crossed her arms out of consternation.

"It can take years, decades, centuries, or maybe never. Let's say you fight Goblins all of your life. You may be an expert at fighting Goblins, but you know nothing about fighting Orcs, Trolls, Were-creatures, or monsters of the elements."

"Elements?" Dain asked.

"You know...creatures of fire, water, air, and stone to name the main four. Then you have all of the Undead, evil humanoids like Dark Elves, Dark Dwarves and Half-Orcs. Then there are Demons, Devils, Witches and Dragons."

This information was overwhelming. There were so many creatures out there they could encounter that were much greater foes than the hundreds of Goblins they'd encountered. How could it be that this was easy? It was enough to make the heartiest warrior reconsider their line of work. Instead of easing their minds, Terelle's explanation was a cause of increased anxiety.

"Dragons?" Dain expressed his concern. "A single

Dragon killed an entire city of Dwarves one time! There were only three survivors and that is because they fled. What's this about Dragons...plural...you mean there are more than one?"

"Relax Dain," Terelle smiled. "I don't see us going off to fight Dragons. It's not like any are known to be in this area. We could always go where some are if you want to give it a try though."

"I think not! Dragons are vicious and intelligent creatures of massive strength. I hope to never even so much as see one alive, thank you!"

"Alright then...we won't pursue Dragon slaying any time soon. How about we slay some food and rest up, right after we poultice-up our wounds?"

"That sounds like a good plan," Dain and Dinly nodded at Trina's acceptance.

It took the companions five days to rest and heal completely, except Splat, who was fine after a single day. Terelle inventoried the new treasure and informed the other group members of their total take.

"Well, we did better this time. It looks to me like these particular Goblins must have been bribed with extra coin to ambush us. We brought back 2,741 zinc rounds and ovals, 1,507 copper, 511 silver, 52 composite, 11 gold, and 2 low quality gems that I'm guessing will be worth about 15 gold for the two of them. We also have another 122 daggers, 39 short swords, and 8 more crossbows with roughly 20 bolts each."

"So, we've done pretty well then, right?" Dinly asked.

"Oh yes," Terelle answered sarcastically. "If we keep this up, we will be rich after only forty to fifty years, as long as we don't need to spend anything."

Dinly looked downtrodden and dejected.

"Don't worry Dinly; we will eventually start picking up some real money once we start fighting harder-to-kill creatures that are more likely to have more of the real currencies. Goblins like shiny objects and I sometimes wonder if they even know the difference between zinc and gold."

"If it's not worth the hassle, then why even bother grabbing it at all?" Trina asked.

"Oh, it's all worth something, and it does add up. It's just heavy and bulky for not much value. It still has some value, so we'll keep gathering what we can because we will eventually need all the coin we can find, even the small stuff."

Terelle flicked back her long, glossy hair after it fell in front of her eyes.

Up until this moment Dain had kept quiet. Taking all

the information and thinking over the value of the different coins and weapons they had gathered.

"You know, the zincs are so small that I might have missed a few while gathering from the bodies I searched. It is sometimes difficult to even notice coins that small."

"We can only gather what we find," Terelle stated. "Maybe I should teach everyone how to search the bodies better, so we don't miss anything. Let's have breakfast and get out of here."

On their trip back to the cavern, Terelle had something she wanted to say, something she hoped wouldn't feed into the fears of the three party members who were just gaining experience.

"You know, we've fought two battles with those Goblins and then come back to the farm to heal. That won't always be possible, and we are going to have to learn to heal as we go at some point. It's not the greatest way to do things, but it does happen...a lot. I wanted you all to realize how it can play out at times."

This was an alarming reality, especially to Trina. She was already unsure of her future as an adventurer. The thought of continually being injured, maybe even more seriously than she'd already been, wasn't a comforting thought. If anything, it instilled a sense of doom and eroded the small hill of confidence she'd built.

As they started getting close, Terelle led them off to their right this time, about a quarter of a mile before they turned left the last time. It was a similar rocky, alpine terrain, but just a different approach to the area.

"We don't want to continue to use the same spots for the horses. The grass will grow thin after a while and the Goblins may figure out that we have horses nearby and take them. They might also start to pattern us."

The companions found another open glade with a small pond. In all actuality, it was a better location than their previous one. They dismounted and picketed the horses where there was plenty of feed and water that would last for as long as they'd planned to be absent. They were venturing back into the cavern, and with any luck they wouldn't walk into another ambush.

This time everybody was much more careful and observant of their surroundings. They never saw any Goblins, just a gray vulture up in the trees that took off when they got too close to it.

The companions looked all around them as they walked through the heavy forest, the lush greenery and tall brown trunks telling an age-old story, if any were willing to listen. Squirrels and birds happily made noises normal for their kind. Even a few rabbits were playing off in the distance, out of reach of even Terelle's archery prowess.

If the companions didn't know better, they would have sworn that this was just a peaceful walk amongst the trees; an outing in the woods. It was a nice feeling, but it was a fantasy and they tried not to be distracted.

Once they had arrived at the mostly clear area where the ambush had taken place, the nice thoughts of a leisurely walk disappeared and were replaced with memories of the battle. The vivid memories were further provoked by all of the bodies that were still strewn about the area of combat. Some had surely been dragged away by scavengers, and others were missing body parts, such as arms and legs and pieces from many of the smaller varieties, but many of the bodies were still right where they had fallen.

Terelle thankfully led them around the carnage, but they could still see it clearly enough, and the smell of death was quite evident. They all went into high alert, making sure weapons and spells were ready to be employed.

9

Taking a roundabout way of getting there, the companions met no Goblins or other denizens. In fact, they never even heard anything out of place. Even the animal life made noises around them, which was completely normal, but seemed peculiar. They arrived at the cave entrance completely unmolested and in wonder. Was this still the same place? Did the companions kill all the Goblins? Or maybe they killed enough of them to make them move away?

Questions, yes. Answers, no. Only time would tell.

Dinly, being small and nimble, was given the job of quickly poking her head in and seeing what she could in the tunnel.

Nothing. Blackness! There weren't any torches burning in the sconces; no light emanating from any source.

She pulled her head back and left the entrance before telling her friends what she saw.

"I couldn't see anything at all beyond the first few feet. There isn't one torch lit and I didn't hear anything at all, either."

"Okay," Terelle said. "I will take point and check for heat signatures. As we pass the torch sconces, check for torches. If they are available, then light them with the torch we will have lit. Keep that torch behind me, so it doesn't interfere with my Infravision. This is where things get scary. We have no idea if they are all gone or have set another trap for us."

Dinly volunteered for torch duty, and the companions set their ranks accordingly. Terelle took the lead, followed by Splat, then Dinly and Trina, and Dain would bring up the rear.

At the first sconce they found that two torches were still in the storage alcove. Dinly lit it with the torch she was carrying and placed it in the sconce. She then grabbed the spare to bring with them.

They left a dimly lit tunnel all the way to the room of the first battle, collecting any extra torches stored among the sconces. A torch in every other sconce was lit, providing enough light to travel by. It also allowed Dinly and Trina to gather in more than a dozen spare torches by the time they arrived at the first large room. Trina carried a large sack with the bulk of the torches in it.

Terelle had still seen no heat sources other than some mice and rats scurrying along the floor. She poked her head through the entry to the room, still seeing no heat signatures. The companions crept into the room. Dinly found two sconces in the room that were staggered and placed burning torches into them.

Except for the blood stains, one would never know of the battle waged here. Apparently, even Goblins had the decency to remove their dead from their living spaces.

After a quick search of the room, which didn't add anything worthwhile, they party headed back into the tunnel and continued down the dank hallway. Terelle was trying her best to not hinder her Infravision, so she stayed a few steps ahead of the others as a practical habit.

Farther into the bowels of the mountain they went. The path was noticeably descending into the earth, although there were sections that were occasionally level.

Closer to Hell, Terelle thought.

The companions came upon another room and applied the same Standard Operating Procedure (SOP) as before. This room was much larger than the first and had two small rooms off it to one side. The two rooms consisted of what was obviously a food preparation room and what was one that probably held food stores. Within the large room there were several crude tables and benches, and it was set up as a dining hall of sorts. Dinly left two torches from her ever-growing surplus burning in this room, as she did in the other large room.

There were several more rooms on both sides of the hallway immediately following the dining hall, and they quickly searched all of them, only finding anything of interest in a storage room. There they found hundreds of torches, a couple dozen wax candles, and a single flint and steel set. They took it all.

"Whoever was here, stripped this place pretty good," Terelle spoke softly and had temporarily changed back to normal vision with the torchlight everywhere. "This at least answers the question of whether we killed them all or not. We did not."

The companions were stopped in a large room with water running through it and a multitude of algae and fungi growing in it. It was damp, bordering on humid, and there was a pinprick of sunlight filtering down from a small hole more than a hundred feet above them.

"The water looks clean where it enters," Terelle commented as she examined the small stream. "We should fill our bellies and flasks while we have a chance...you never know where the next watering hole will be."

"We must have come at least a mile or more by now," Dain stated, familiar with distance underground. "I wonder how far this tunnel goes?"

"Well, there's only one way to find out," Terelle answered and then waved the others back behind her to change back to Infravision and continue down the tunnel.

****

Back at the cave entrance, a sizzling sound, at first loud and then fading, echoed down the tunnel as the first torch was smothered by a wet cloth. Footsteps moved toward the next torch.

There were three large Humanoids with grey skin that was patchy with yellowish spots of different shapes and sizes. Each spot was bulbous and protruded from the body enough to be noticeable to any who saw them. The long hair-like tentacles that sprouted from their torsos were a darker gray than the skin and hung from an inch to a foot long in an indiscernible pattern.

The creatures had four eyes, two in front, like most Humanoids, and one on each side close to where the ears would be on a Human. They had ears in the back of their heads with flaps that spread from the base of the skull to just above the collar muscles.

They were around six feet tall and muscular. And despite their appearance, they were somewhat intelligent; definitely smarter than any Goblin. Each of them carried a nasty looking mace with sharp, rusty metal points all around the business end. They were called Knobbers.

Behind them walked a Humanish looking lady in a hooded cloak that just showed a few tendrils of her fiery red hair. Her long pointy nose and sunken green eyes, mostly hidden by the hood, didn't help her appearance any.

She carried a staff that was a knotty affair with a blood-red ruby set in the top and was surrounded by prickly briars. The only other notable feature about her was that she appeared to glide along the floor, not really taking any noticeable steps.

The four of them kept a steady pace as they continued down the tunnel, seemingly not in any kind of hurry.

****

The companions came to a fork in the tunnel and had to make a decision about which way to go.

"Both are well traveled...look," Terelle pointed out the worn floor going each way as she started to teach Dinly how to track underground. "If you pay attention, you can just see that the left offshoot has been used most recently from this direction."

"There is a fine layer of dust to the right, along the edges here," she now showed specific spots along the edge of the tunnel, "And here, and here. If you look closely at the left tunnel you won't see any of this dust. This means that they evacuated to the left."

"I think I've got it," Dinly said.

"Good, because you will get to try it at the next intersection," Terelle informed her.

"Okay," Dinly announced with more assuredness than she really felt.

Terelle led them all a few hundred yards to the next intersection where Dinly would get her chance to interpret the tracks.

"Okay, you're up."

Dinly knelt down with her torch and investigated each of the three directions tracks could possibly go in the four-way intersection.

"It looks as if they turned right, but there are some signs of traffic going forward."

"Very good," Terelle looked pleased. "There could be any number of reasons for a few heading in that direction, but we should follow the main pack of them as this will likely lead us to wherever they are planning to stop and harass people up top trying to live their lives."

So, they continued to follow the main group of Goblins. Interestingly enough, this path is where the torches and sconces stopped. Trina started to carry a second lit torch to expand the area of light and to have at least one torch lit when the other was burned out. Dinly, Dain, and Trina carried spares in any pockets that would hold them because the sack was overflowing. They didn't dare leave any torch behind since they had no idea how long they would need artificial light.

Terelle had Dinly look for signs of passage at three more intersections before they noticed a dim light ahead in the distance.

With everyone now on a heightened state of alert, the other companions instantly froze when Terelle used a hand signal to stop. She gathered them around.

"There's a pit trap right in front of where I was standing, and we will have to stay two feet to the left of the walkway to go around it. We will go one at a time after we rope off, just in case someone falls. Splat, you'll need to fly over it...we could never hold your weight if you fall in."

"Okay!" Splat replied.

"Won't these torches give us away?" Trina asked.

"I'm hoping that by us approaching as if we belong here, that the Goblins might think we are some of their kind showing up from the other tunnel," Terelle explained.

The companions used a fifty foot rope to tie each other together into one long chain, including Splat, who used the flight capability of his boots to levitate and move forward at the same speed as the others. With Splat using magic to fly, it was very unlikely that anyone would be lost, even if the pit was deep.

As they were getting ready to continue, Dinly asked,

"Can we look in the pit? There might be something of interest down there."

"I doubt it would be worth the effort, and it would take valuable time. Plus, we might not be able to reset the trap if we trip it. So, no... I don't think we should," Terelle answered.

"I'm sure I can reset it. Can I please look down there?" Dinly whined.

"Okay, very well, but let's be quick about it," Terelle relented.

"Thank you!"

Dinly easily tripped the trap without falling in and asked Trina for her torch. She looked down into the expertly dug pit and described what she saw.

"The pit is only about ten feet down, and there are a few spikes embedded in the bottom. Impaled on the spikes are a Goblin, a Human and another Humanoid creature. There are weapons and other gear in the pit, and I can hear water down there...and I see two openings we could easily walk through."

Terelle curiously looked down into the pit, remarking, "How interesting. Notice how spread out the spikes are?"

"Uh huh." Dinly acknowledged.

"If someone climbed down along the corners, they'd be safe from the spikes...even Splat could fit without getting hurt," Terelle took a moment to think out loud. "If you want to search down there, I won't stop you. But you need to make it quick, okay?"

Dinly excitedly nodded and tied off with the last ten feet of the rope before descending.

"Okay, drop me a torch."

Trina did so and Dinly picked up the torch, carefully avoiding anything combustible, then she looked around. Through one of the openings she could see an underground river going by only fifteen feet from her through a natural opening. The tunnel was maybe seven feet long before opening into a cavern where the river cut through it.

Next, she looked opposite the first opening and could tell that this second opening was cut by man or Dwarf. The sides were smooth and nearly exact, and she could see from the dim light thrown from the Goblin torch, it was a tunnel that went back at least twenty feet.

Not seeing or hearing anything down there with her other than the river, she quickly searched the bodies of the dead, leaving a broken crossbow, but grabbing the other weapons, valuables, and useful items. After only a minute, she climbed back up the rope and handed her findings to Terelle.

Dinly reset the trap, untied from the end of the rope, and then retied in her original spot. While doing this, she explained what she had found.

Terelle passed a two-handed sword to Splat to carry and added three more daggers to the ever-growing pile in her large belt pouch. There were three small purses, and she kept the contents of the two that hadn't come from the Human. The last purse she gave to Dinly for finding the loot in the first place and for retrieving everything.

Dinly looked pleased with herself.

Terelle then placed the small sack of odds and ends into her pack to check out later. The party moved forward beyond the pit and then untied from each other. It was now time to figure out what lay before them.

It was only a couple of hundred feet or so beyond the pit to where the glow came from. From where she was standing, Terelle could see that it was a small room, with two double bunks, a table, and four chairs. Two torch sconces with lit torches brightened things enough for her to see the room, its contents, and the four Humanoid creatures sitting in those chairs.

Terelle wasn't stupid enough to just walk into the room, or to pass this room and continue down the tunnel. As she approached the entry to this room, she handed Dain her torch and snuck up on the opening to take a peek inside. She then backed away and retreated the last ten feet back to her companions.

She whispered, "There is a small room with four orcs inside that are playing cards at a table. If we go in fast and fighting, they might not get to their weapons."

"Doorway looks small," Splat whispered

"Unfortunately, it is too small...so, you watch the tunnel. You three come with me and be ready for a fight."

"I'll get the one with his back to us," Dinly announced quietly.

"Okay, now let's go!" Terelle commanded.

The companions snuck up on the room with weapons drawn, then all, but Splat, rushed in and immediately attacked the Orcs.

An Orc facing them started to stand as Terelle ran toward him. A bow would have been easier, but the room was too small, and she didn't want to inadvertently shoot one of her friends. So, sword play it was to be.

Dinly ran toward her target with a short sword over her head, pointing down. Dain closed on the Orc on the left, and Trina cast a spell at the one on the right just as he started to stand.

To his credit, the Orc facing Terelle was able to bring his mace into play. The two of them went back and forth, their weapons clashing, while all around them Orcs began to fall.

Dinly buried her short sword into the Orc's back that

was in front of her. Dain cut a good chunk of the side from the one he faced, the large section of torso coming away from its owner with a splatter of blood, muscle, and bone. That Orc collapsed sideways and bled out quickly.

Trina used a spell that held her Orc in place, almost as if he were paralyzed. This was the first time she had used this particular spell in combat. She had no idea what an Orc was and figured that holding it in place would give her time to assess the situation better.

Once Dinly managed to pull her blade from her target, she noticed an unmoving Orc and Terelle locked in combat with another. She chose to run to the right, passing the frozen-in-place Orc and swung her blade with all of her might at the back of the legs belonging to the Orc Terelle was fighting.

With a shriek, the Orc fell like a stone, albeit, a very mad and surprised stone. Terelle easily finished him off after that, while Dinly deftly plunged her blade into the back of the Orc that was frozen in place.

Trina looked miffed and complained to Dinly, "I was just getting ready to take him out!"

"Think of it this way," Dinly said with a smile while freeing her sword, "I saved you from using a spell...You'll have an extra for later."

"Yeah, I guess you're right," Trina agreed.

"What do we have out there?" Terelle asked Splat.

"Nothing either way."

"Okay, friends, let's check for treasure...but no more large weapons at this time, unless they look very special."

Everyone listened to Terelle and took just the small stuff. They handed all the items they gathered, as they had before, to Terelle.

"I hate leaving weapons behind, but we can only carry so much bulk." Terelle reassessed the situation and instructed, "Put the weapons in a sack. We will bring it with us for now but keep an eye out for a stashing place."

Dinly looked around for a second before they left and commented, "You know...it was one of these Orcs that I saw in the pit with the Goblin and Human. When I saw the body, I didn't know what it was. Now I know! So, thank you for that knowledge."

"You're welcome, Dinly, but we need to move on."

"How about these bodies?" Dain asked.

"Leave them...we need to go," Terelle stated. "I have a bad feeling that we just stepped into a major snake pit."

None the worse for wear, the companions continued down the tunnel for a couple hundred more feet, where it branched right, as well as continued its forward progression. Dinly looked at the signs of traffic in the dirt.

"It shows that both directions are definitely used...but

there is more forward use than there is to the right."

To be sure, Terelle looked for herself.

"That is true, however, the smaller footprints lead to the right, so we should also go that way."

The party continued to the right. It took them mere minutes to start finding other passages, mostly branching off to their right. There was only one passage that led to their left, but it was a large passage, capable of accommodating three Splats side by side. At this intersection they had to be extra stealthy, as they had no idea what else could be around.

Once past that intersection, the passages on the right became more frequent and it looked to Terelle as if small groups and individuals had veered off from the main group of Goblins and went down these passageways.

At the seventh of these, Terelle brought the companions into the passageway quickly and took them eighty feet inward.

"What's going on?" Trina asked.

"The Goblins are splitting off as if they were going home," Terelle answered. "On top of that, I think I saw a Goblin up ahead of us, so we needed to get off of that main tunnel."

"What do we do now?" Dain asked.

"We clear out this tunnel and go from there," she

answered.

The companions pulled their weapons and proceeded to follow the recent footprints of the Goblins. After another twisting three hundred feet, the tunnel opened up into a small cavern that had three exits. This room had a couple of barrels along one wall, some seating arrangements of stone around a fire pit, and a couple of sconces filled with unlit torches. There was nothing living in the room except for the companions.

They went through the left of the three openings and found a bedroom of sorts with a couple of deer-hide rugs with sleeping Goblins piled upon them. One of the creatures looked like those who they had been fighting, and the other was obviously different. There were also a few other small items of "furniture," but nothing that looked like it had any value.

Terelle motioned for Dinly to quietly join her in an attempt to dispatch the Goblins as quietly as possible.

Silently, the two women successfully eliminating these two enemies. The bodies were quickly searched and a few items with very little value were retrieved. There was an opening from the room that operated like a window of sorts. It looked out over a valley that was filled with other openings, and there was an occasional Orc or Goblin that could be seen in their homes, so everyone stayed back from the opening to keep others from seeing them. They searched the dead Goblins' bedding and found a small purse hidden underneath the nasty hides. They grabbed it before exiting the "Home."

The next room contained two more Goblins in the same kind of bedding, and even though the female woke up at the last second, it was too late, and both were silenced forever. As before, they searched the room with similar results. The party, once again, avoided the window that looked out into the valley as they searched and left. It was becoming clear that it was nighttime for these creatures.

As they moved on, the last room they encountered had no occupants and it appeared that it was only a storage area for foodstuffs, kitchen equipment of a very basic nature, and a few other worthless odds and ends. There wasn't anything worth taking, so they chose to leave and head back the other direction.

The companions backtracked through four of the previous entrances with the same results before things changed. At the sixth tunnel, a Goblin in the first room wasn't asleep and before it could be permanently silenced it was able to call out an alarm.

Two Goblins in the next room woke up to the sound and sounded an alarm that rang through the valley, notifying all of the inhabitants of the intruders. This was a dangerous situation that could easily turn deadly for the party.

Making quick work of the two Goblins before running to within twenty feet of the main tunnel, they grabbed the purses that were visible. They didn't even bother looking for other treasure.

Out of the very first tunnel the companions had passed, at the place where Terelle started to notice Goblins peeling off, two Goblins rushed down the passage and spotted Terelle looking their direction. One of them saw her and noticed she was not from around there. The beasts sounded an alarm before they both charged Terelle's direction.

By the time they had arrived at her position, the other companions had joined her. Terelle and Dain met the Goblins and made quick work of them both. Unfortunately, many more creatures could be heard coming towards them from the direction they hadn't finished exploring. They hadn't planned for this, and realized they were dealing with potentially dire circumstances.

Terelle quickly snagged the purses and daggers of the dead, and then told the others to follow her. She ran quickly back from the direction they had originally come from. The best thing they could do now was to find a place to hide. First things first was getting there.

They reached the large hallway, now on their right side,

and could hear commotion from it, but they spotted no creature at the intersection. They ran through as Trina lit another torch before the one Terelle was carrying faded.

"Thanks!" Terelle said as she grabbed the new torch from behind her and continued running.

Torchlight up ahead told them that they had company and they would have to fight their way through. Not noticing anyone behind them, Terelle had Dain and Splat take the front. She and Trina would be at the rear of the party, and Dinly would watch their backs. Terelle set down her torch, grabbed her bow, and pulled two arrows from her quiver. Trina placed the torch on the ground against a wall and readied a spell. The wait was only a few seconds long.

Once she was certain of her targets, Terelle quickly launched one arrow, and then another, at the two Orcs in front. As she pulled two more arrows, fire shot from the fingertips of Trina's hands, and small little missiles of fire hit one of the Orcs and it dropped. Two more arrows and one more spell later, there were a total of six less Orcs coming when the mass collided with Splat and Dain.

Dain was hit several times but didn't show any injuries. Splat was hit many more times, but he kept on killing. The companions had to back up several times because of the piles of dead that were stacking up. Splat and Dain were racking up bodies, while Terelle unsheathed her sword and was ready to use it on any who made it through.

As the Orc attack petered out, Terelle called out to her friends, "Grab any purses you see as we climb over the dead...let's go!"

She and Trina grabbed the torches.

They all quickly stripped purses from as many of the Orcs as could be easily grabbed, and then ran as fast as they could. There was no time to linger. It wasn't long before something rushed toward them head on.

It was a massive creature, easily the size of Splat. He took the forefront, swinging his maul for all he was worth as they met. Splat missed and hit the wall, knocking chips of rock to the floor as the creature connected Splat's right arm with one of its fists.

Splat noticed the punch actually hurt and became mad. He lifted the maul from the floor and tossed it at the monster. As it landed, the tunnel shook, and the monster screamed in pain from the impact of the maul landing on its foot. Then Splat started punching the monster with continuous right and left swings, beating the monster to a bloody pulp and cracking its skull several times. He lost track of time.

Dinly announced that there were Goblins coming from behind. The group needed to reset their defense.

"Splat! Enough, we need you!" Terelle called out to

Splat.

He turned and saw a horde of Goblins coming. With ease he picked up his maul in one hand and the body of the monster in the other, squeezing through his friends to join Dain at the front line. Dinly grabbed the monster's heavy purse as Splat carried the body by her. Their positions were reversed in the tunnel and she was, once again, watching their backs.

If the Orcs had numbers, the Goblins had more. They had already witnessed this fact and braced for the worst.

Splat started the battle by launching the monster's body against the first wave of attacking creatures. The monster's body smashed several of them, and then the companions went to work. They killed dozens of Goblins, and then backed up. Dozens more would fall, then they would back up again. At least this time they were going the correct direction. The real problem was that some of the Goblins got through and were able to injure Trina, Terelle, and even Dinly.

Dain and Splat, too, were noticeably injured when the last few Goblins fled the scene of the battle. Terelle told the others to only grab purses from the bodies nearby, and then the companions started walking and limping away.

As they got farther along, Splat started feeling better, but it was to be short lived as another kind of large creature appeared before them. This creature and Splat went at it for a couple of minutes, battling in a primitive dance, before Splat got the upper hand because Dain saw a target of opportunity and struck the creature's leg. Dain was kicked aside for his efforts, crashing against a wall and sliding down to the floor unconscious.

With effort, the companions dragged past the large corpse. Dinly grabbed the creature's large and heavy purse. Splat was carrying Dain.

Within sixty feet of the last battle, they came to the pit. Terelle looked at her companions and decided.

"We are going into the pit for a while. Get the rope."

Dinly tripped the trap and opened it for the others. Splat helped the others down, and then used his boots to float to the bottom of the pit. Afterwards he lifted Dinly into the air so she could reset the trap. Luckily, no enemies had come to bother them. The beaten up and ragged group dragged themselves, or were carried in the case of Dain, to the area with the river in it.

Once they had passed the entrance, they could see an old wooden dock going out into the water. Two old, sunken boats were on each side of the structure. To their left was a dilapidated hut, and another one stood a short distance beyond that one. To their right was a more stoutly built home that was constructed of rocks and had a wooden roof.

Everything looked to be long-deserted and in need of repair.

The badly banged up troop worked their way to the rock house and looked inside. There was a man sitting in a chair at a table. The man had been dead for decades, at least, for he was now only a skeleton in a few strips of clothing.

In the dusty, cobweb-filled home were a chest, two beds, and the weapons of the man at the table. Hanging from his skeletal figure was a longsword and a dagger, both in their respective scabbards. There was also a shiny metal shield hanging upon a wall.

The companions started checking each other's wounds. Dain had a pretty severe cut between two of his armor plates and a head wound to worry about. He was definitely not going to make it without help. Terelle pulled out a potion and had him drink it. Instantly, Dain felt better, and the wound closed. His head started healing a bit, but he was still far from being completely healed.

First aid was administered to all, including Splat, and then they consumed a quick meal. Everyone, except Terelle, then went to sleep.

10

Four hours after Splat went to sleep, he woke up and took over on watch, letting Terelle and the others sleep for at least eight hours while he was on watch.

When everyone finally woke up, it was bathroom calls, cleaning bandages, another meal, and more sleep by all as Terelle and Splat split the watch.

After two full days of this with no interruptions, the companions started feeling like they might actually live. Terelle used the torches sparingly, making them last as long as possible. In the downtime, she went through the purses, including the two big ones that Dinly had snagged. Dinly, the adept thief she was turning into, was also able to disarm the trap to the chest in the stone house and unlock it. Opening it, she found seven vials of liquid, many coins, several gems, two pieces of jewelry, and a crown and a scepter. It was after Dinly had finally opened the chest, that Dain found the key in the dirt, right under the dead man's body just to the side of the chair.

Terelle looked at the coins and noticed that they were from a previous empire that used to control this area, as well as vast amounts of other kingdoms that popped up after its fall. Most of the coins had been melted down when the kingdom fell, which might make these coins worth more than usual. The crown and scepter may have also had something to do with the old empire but finding that out would take some research. If the companions could escape these tunnels and get to safety with this chest full of history, they might be well on their way to putting their plan into motion.

Another point of interest in the house were the weapons and the shield that were left behind. Considering how long they had been there, especially near the waterfront, they should have been at least dull looking, if not down-right rusty. Yet, here they were all nice and shiny. Even the scabbards were in perfect condition. At the very least, the leather should be old and brittle, but it, as well, was in immaculate condition. Terelle suspected all of them were magical, and they were as important to bring with them as the chest full of treasure was.

Terelle was becoming worried about her new friends. Each had sustained several injuries that would still take many days to heal. Perhaps more days than they had food for, even if it was rationed. Unfortunately, rationing the food would only slow the healing process. They would need to leave while they still had a supply of food.

The last thing that needed to be examined were the vials in the chest. Terelle wondered if any of them would heal her friends, but all the vials were very old and would have to be checked out closely. She knew the four blue potions should be for healing or water breathing, the green one should be a poison or a potion for the curing of a disease, the yellow one should be a cure for lycanthropy, and the red should be for fire resistance or fire breathing. Knowing what they should be didn't mean she was correct, and she could be terribly wrong. Terelle wasn't ready to take such a risk, especially with her friends' lives.

She did at least have one more potion that was on the dead Human from the spikes. It was in the correct bottle and of the correct hue of blue, so she could tell it was a healing potion. But with only one, she decided to save it for an emergency.

For three more days the companions stayed where they were and healed to a degree. Now, with only one day of food left, they needed to get moving. Only Splat was completely healed. Even Terelle needed another week to recuperate fully, and she was in the best shape of all of them except for Splat. Sore and still slightly injured, the companions put on their gear and picked up their packs and weapons. A few party members who felt strong enough carried the items deemed important, like the shield and weapons from the rock house. Splat, with his incredible strength restored, easily carried the reclosed chest. They all headed back to the spiked pit area.

Splat set down the chest long enough to pick up Dinly. She listened for any traffic from up above before disengaging the trap. Hearing nothing, she looked both directions for torchlight and saw none.

"I think we are okay," she whispered down to the others.

Terelle used the one lit torch to light another that she gave Trina. It was one of only two spares left.

If only we had been able to bring that sack of torches we were carrying around for so long, Terelle thought. *At least we still have the sack of weapons."*

Splat lifted each companion up to the tunnel before grabbing the chest and sack filled with blades and flying out.

With everyone clear of the pit, Dinly then reset the trap before they all started out.

Based on information from Dinly's new tracking knowledge, and backed by Terelle making sure of Dinly's findings, the party turned one way or the other when at an intersection. Terelle didn't like what she saw. There seemed to be much more traffic heading in the same direction they needed to travel. Regretfully, they had limited choices in the matter as to where they could go. Their need for food and rest dictated their path.

After hours of traveling, Terelle had to use her last torch, and while they were stopped for those few seconds, she thought she heard noises from behind them. The noises sounded like very faint drums of some sort. This was troubling to Terelle.

"We need to move quickly!" she exclaimed in a whisper.

They picked up the pace as much as they could without making excessive noise, and they were able to maintain that pace for nearly twenty minutes before they noticed torch light ahead of them.

Terelle slowed the companions to a normal walk to let them all regain some of their energy in case a fight was near. Minutes later they started passing sconces on the walls with lit torches in them, and they recognized that they were in the old Goblin area they had first encountered.

They started getting close to the first room when several Orcs came out of the room to face them. One Orc looked at the chest Splat was carrying and then spoke in the common language.

"You thought you had outsmarted us by finding someplace to hide. But we knew you would have to try and leave sometime. I must say, thank you for bringing us a chest full of treasure. I'm sure that whatever is in there will help fund our armies in the near future. Now, unfortunately for you, we must kill you."

"How do you speak our language?" Terelle asked quickly, stalling for time and possibly information.

"In case you haven't noticed, Elf, I'm only half-Orc and I have lived amongst your racist people for years as a mercenary. Now if you want, you can surrender, and I'm sure I can arrange for a proper hanging. Otherwise we must kill you all much more slowly."

Dain moved forward as if surrendering so he could stand next to Splat, who was setting down the chest and letting go of the sack of weapons. Once in place, Dain said a short but interesting comment.

"Slime buckets, come and try to take me!"

The half-Orc pointed to the companions and ordered, "Get them!"

Splat and Dain moved forward, swinging their weapons. The Orcs didn't stand a chance. Within a couple of minutes, all fourteen, including the half-Orc, were dead.

As soon as the fighting had stopped, the companions heard a commotion in front of them and looked toward it. Orcs poured out of all the other rooms.

Dain looked at Splat and said, "You kill those on the

left, I'll kill those on the right!"

"Good!" Splat replied.

Terelle took up position to the rear of them, set to the middle, wishing she still had some arrows to let fly. Trina and Dinly had been holding the torches, but now set them down. Dinly pulled her short sword and Trina readied a spell.

This time, the two party members in front wouldn't be able to do all the work in a blur of motion. The Orcs advanced with hatred in their black, beady little eyes. The small army started at a march until they reached within one hundred feet. With a roar, the mass began to charge the companions.

Splat and Dain took advantage of the short break to regain some stamina and they waited for the Orcs to reach them.

With the first wave crashing into them, fierce fighting ensued. Some of the Orcs made it past the front line, finding the biting blades of steel belonging to Terelle and Dinly. Trina used spell after spell until she had no more.

As the battle raged on, Trina resorted to using her dagger when an Orc got through Terelle and Dinly. She did this time and again until Dinly went down under a clubbing blow from an Orc that had breached their defenses. Trina used her dagger to stab the Orc in the neck when he was getting ready to finish Dinly off. After pulling the dagger from the Orc's thick skin, Trina picked up Dinly's short sword and stood her ground against two more Orcs that fought their way through. She didn't come out of it unscathed. Trina sustained cuts to her left arm and right leg before she, too, succumbed to her injuries.

By this time, Terelle was barely able to stand and fight, running on adrenaline alone. Dain was trying to get back up from a fifth fall to the floor, and Splat looked like he had been through a blade factory after having tried each blade on his body. Splat was still up and fighting the last few Orcs when one of them made it past him and rammed Terelle off her feet. The Orc got up. Terelle didn't. He raised his weapon above his head to strike Terelle dead, when a dagger flew through the air and stuck him in the chest. Though not enough to kill the Orc, it did catch his attention enough to make him hesitate. That was all the time Splat needed to smash in his side with one final swing.

There were no more Orcs.

Every one of the companions was covered in blood, sweat and, pieces of their enemy. Splat went to Terelle and checked to see if she still lived. After checking her pulse, like she had recently shown him, he seemed satisfied enough to check on the others. When he went to Trina, he noticed her dagger was missing.

"Thank you for saving Terelle...now I need to save all of you," Splat said while tears rolled down through the blood covering his face.

He first wrapped a shirt around Trina's leg wound, which was bleeding badly, and then her arm. He next went to Dain, where he bandaged the wound in the Dwarf's gut. He came back to Terelle and dropped to the ground, exhausted. Splat sat on the ground and held Terelle's head in his lap, cradling her while sobbing.

11

Terelle opened her eyes and saw Splat crying through a mask of blood and Orc flesh. She was afraid to ask but had to know.

"Have we been captured? Oh, my head is killing me."

"You do live," Splat announced. "I did what I can, but it is not enough. The others are hurt bad...real bad this time."

Terelle shook the cobwebs from her head, instantly regretting it. She almost blacked back out but managed to stay conscious.

"Who is still able to move?"

"Only me and not much."

Terelle took in the situation, then heard the distant beating of the drums sending a shiver of alarm throughout her body.

"We have to get out of here! Help me up."

With Splat's help, Terelle got to her feet. Though slightly dizzy, she checked on the others. She then took the healing potion and gave it to Dain, who could barely breathe.

"Here, drink this. It will help a little."

Dain took the potion and it seemed to bring him back

from death's door, healing his gut injury enough to move him, but not enough for him to move on his own.

She next went to Trina, examined her condition, and regretfully said, "I don't have any way to knowingly heal you. I can grab a potion from the chest, but I'm not sure if it will help you. You need to tell me if you want to take the chance. If it works you might live...if it doesn't, you'll surely die."

"I'll take the chance."

Terelle retrieved a blue potion and brought it back to Trina. When Trina drank it down, it had no visible effects. Perhaps it needed time. Meanwhile, Terelle went to Dinly and bandaged a few cuts on her. She was unconscious and most of her damage looked to be from a head wound. Having done all she could, Terelle collapsed to the floor.

Splat then had an idea. He got up and checked the nearest room, finding a table and several bunk beds. Hearing the drums slowly getting closer, he took the table and lay it upside down on the floor of the tunnel, just past all the bodies of the Orcs.

He then brought two of the beds and set them where they would be at an angle with heads raised and feet lowered. One foot end of the bed was laid inside the head end of the other. He then loaded his companions on the beds, two per bed and placed the chest and sack of weapons on the table. Using his rope, he tied the table so that he could put the rope around himself and pull the whole set-up. Before leaving, he retrieved his companions' weapons and placed them with the companions they belonged to. By the time he finished all of this, he could hear the drums quite a bit louder.

Splat was torn. He wanted to go kill those who had done this to his friends, until they were all dead, but he knew he must get his friends to safety. Besides, he was already severely hurt and exhausted himself. His friends had to come first.

Dinly regained consciousness when Splat went to get her. Since he was dragging his friends to the beds and working to the point of near exhaustion, she was able to snag a few purses and weapons while she was passing the dead Orcs. She could barely move one of her arms and her head, which throbbed something horrible.

With everything and everyone loaded, Splat started pulling the whole ensemble as fast as he could in his present state of disrepair. When Splat finally reached the end of the tunnel, he dropped the torch he had brought and went outside to see if there was an ambush waiting for him and his friends. He didn't see any, so he squeezed back through the entrance and brought his friends outside, one at a time, carrying them as he regained a portion of his strength and stamina.

Once his friends were outside, he brought out the chest and sack of weapons, then his carrying platform, one piece at a time. He reassembled the whole thing and tied it together with more rope as he would no longer be dragging it along a solid rock floor, but uneven ground with rocks, tree roots, and soft spots in the soil.

He went back in to extinguish the torch when he was attacked by several Goblins. He didn't have his maul, so he fought them all with his fists, raining death and destruction on all seven of them without even one getting by him.

Splat could hear more coming, and knew he couldn't get his friends to safety in time, so he squeezed through the opening, ran over to where his friends were and grabbed his maul, then squeezed back into the tunnel with only seconds to spare. It was up to him and him alone, there would be no help. He was the last hope his friends had of staying alive. Failure wasn't an option, more so now than ever.

He swung his deadly maul with a vengeance. No way were these vile creatures going to get his friends, not while he could still fight. His determination was driven by his loyalty and his rage.

Unfortunately, there were more than forty of them and only one of him. Try as he might, on two occasions, one of the little creatures got passed him. This was an all-out war.

Even the drummer dropped his drum and attacked with a dagger. Splat furiously dealt death to them all and then rushed outside to kill the two creatures that had escaped the tunnel. He hoped he wouldn't find his friends all dead.

When he exited the cave, he saw two dead Goblins and a swaying Dinly with a new wound from her efforts.

"Are there any more?" she weakly asked as she saw Splat.

"No, not right now."

"Good!" She then fell back to the ground.

****

Splat pushed with all the remaining strength he had before the boulder ground into place, blocking the cave entrance. With any luck, the barrier would stop any creature long enough for the companions to escape the area. With that task done, he went over to Dinly and bandaged her new cut, noticing that she had grabbed the purses and daggers from the two Goblins she'd killed. He laid her on the bed before laying on the ground himself for nearly a half hour, then sitting back up. Some of his energy had been restored, but he could tell his rejuvenating power was used up for a while.

"Time to go!" he said.

Only Terelle was awake when he spoke.

"If you can get us to the horses, we can make it back by nightfall."

"Ugh! Horses gone or starving by now."

"Yeah...you're probably right."

"Am right, now I pull."

Pull he did. As he struggled along, the legs of the back bed caught several times on roots, rocks, and ruts until he broke them off. It was much easier after that, and he found that he left less of a trail without the legs. After what felt like hours, he finally made it to where the horses had been picketed. They were gone. With a grunt of "I told you so" to a now unconscious Terelle, he aimed for the farm the best he could remember.

Once out of the hills and with the trees thinning, he found he was nearly a half mile off course and made the correction.

Throughout this time, there were occasions when Dinly, Terelle, or Dain would wake up and ask for water, or where they were. But for the most part, Splat was all alone as he hauled the companions, treasure, and weapons closer to the widow's farm. By the time he pulled into the farm it was well past midnight. A large grey vulture, like the one they'd seen before, whisked through the air above the companions, floating on the wind.

With very little strength left, Splat was ready to drop by the time he dragged the group into the farm's yard. He hated to do it, but he went to the door of the house and knocked.

It took a few minutes and a couple of more knocks, but the old widow finally opened the door.

"Do you know what time it…Oh the gods! What has happened to you?"

"Not me, my friends," he teared up. "I can't help them no more, can you?"

"Yes, I'll do what I can," she said.

Splat's eyes rolled back in his head and he fell to the ground, his maul falling from his hand and denting the ground with a thud.

****

Three ugly creatures walked up to the now sealed entrance and looked it over. An ugly Human-looking woman floated behind them.

"Grug hust garg!" one of the creatures uttered.

"Don't worry my pets...we might have gotten here too late this time, but they will be back. Well, most of them will."

ABOUT THE AUTHORS

Jeff R. Smith now lives in Idaho. It's been years since his last release due to an extensive move, medical issues, and setting up his family's homestead. He still finds time to write around his busy schedule and has started catching up enough to do the dastardly work of editing and the other details of releasing books. He has teamed up with lifelong friend Richard Roux and artist Emilie Beck for the fantasy series that starts with this book you are now reading.

Richard Roux—teacher, historian, author—lives in Bakersfield, California. He has stepped away from his comfort zone of researching and writing non-fiction and historical fiction to venture into the fantasy realm.

Emilie Beck is a student in Bakersfield, CA. She hopes to have a career in game design. She can be found as TheMilkPrince on Instagram and YouTube.

OTHER BOOKS BY THE AUTHORS

Jeff R. Smith:

*Into Oblivion: Part 1—A Place to Call Home
(Limited Edition Pre-Release)*

Into Oblivion

Preparations

Richard Roux:

*Bootleggers, Booze, and Busts: Prohibition in Kern County,
1919-1933*

A Branch Too Weak

A Good Stock

9 780578 591841